" **N** ice ch[...]
are [...]
you?"

She lifted me off the ground and placed me in the Geek's hands. With his usual showmanship, he lifted me melodramatically high above his head, held me there dangling head down, then slowly lowered me toward his open mouth. I did my part, twisting and flapping my wings, and squawked at the top of my lungs in faked panic as his mouth came closer and closer. Teamwork is an important part of any act and I didn't want to blow it for him by becoming blasé. Once my head brushed past his teeth, however, I became motionless. Now that he couldn't swallow castor oil it was especially dangerous to move or even twitch. I didn't want a repeat of what happened the day of the Great Hard-On. I was still having nightmares about that.

THE GEEK

TINY ALICE

MASQUERADE BOOKS, INC.
801 SECOND AVENUE
NEW YORK, N.Y. 10017

First Masquerade Edition 1995

First Printing October 1995

ISBN 1-56333-341-4

Cover Photograph © 1995 by Robert Chouraqui

Cover Design by Dayna Navaro

Manufactured in the United States of America
Published by Masquerade Books, Inc.
801 Second Avenue
New York, N.Y. 10017

To:
Harlan Ellison and Norman Spinrad
who thought of the Geek
and Hank Stine
who thought of the chicken
and to Lenny
who started the whole thing by accident.

Chapter 1

Being swallowed makes me horny.

It always did. What's even worse, I'm on the road with no females. Life without a woman is a drag. And friend, if the circus seems sunny, sandy, and swinging, forget it. It's a bummer.

Here I am, an old hand, a trooper since I was a chick, and let me tell you, being Cock of the Roost is good only if there is a roost to cock. What I mean, see, is that I've been part of the swallowing act as far back as I can remember.

The Geek is okay, and so is the circus, if that's

your scene. But my Geek, he's poor and so is the circus. He uses one chicken, one flaming sword, and one yo-yo. That's all. And I'm the only chicken in the circus, the whole fucking circus. No hens.

I'm getting to be a rooster, and what they say about roosters is true, every word of it. You remember the song?

We had a milk cow
No milk would she give
We had a milk cow
No milk would she give
My wife said, "Honey, it ain't funny
We're losing money
We have a milk cow
That gives no milk."
One day a rooster came into our yard,
And caught old Bessie off her guard
Now she's giving egg nog
Just like she used to
Ever since that rooster came into our yard.

The last verse is about the farmer's wife. People laugh, but that's the way we are. So here I am, ready and able, but no one is willing. I could leave but the circus is in my blood.

Go to another circus, you say, one with a hen? That's easily said, but circuses stay as far apart as they can, and I'd starve before I found the closest one. And if I didn't, I might get there to find they had no hen. But if they had no geek, I'd be in real trouble. I'd be out of a job.

That's the problem with specialization. You're limited. My specialty is being swallowed. I'm tops in my field. I know every pitfall in the trade. You have to be still going in. If you wiggle, you may hurt the Geek and be swallowed for good during the convulsions. An occupational hazard, but a real one: I've seen many a chicken go to his reward that way...and it's a hell of a reward to go to.

Well, this sex thing is driving me crazy. Here I am at my sexual peak, and nothing to "peak" with. I've tried everything, but when the old dangler gets tight and heavy I really feel it. I've tried rubbing it against the tent rope. I've tried coke bottles. It's all been the same; nothing. And the next morning, ouch!

I have found something that helps—not much, but it helps.

Sometimes, by accident, of course, walking into a tent at almost any hour of the day or night, I happen on couples making it. Watching them arouses the same feeling in me, laying it on harder and tighter and hotter until it all shoots out—a milky, sticky fountain. A kind of flaming free and cool feeling, rolling down your legs, matting feathers and making them sticky and stiff. But it leaves you feeling good, *good, GOOD.*

9

The process still has bugs in it, though.

I was being swallowed.

It's difficult to describe. First he grabs you by the legs and clenches them tightly together. You're supposed to struggle—it's part of the act. You have to put on a show for the suckers. Put one over on them and they'll love you for it, so I really lay it on thick. I squawk—I flap my wings—I shake my thing. They really get worked up.

There are all sorts of tricks to the game; like ruffling your feathers before going in to make yourself look bigger, then folding down smooth and tight and stiff as you are inserted. If you're lucky and it's a good geek, the passage will be slicked down with "natural body juices," as they say. If the opening is dry, you're in real trouble and so is the geek. It hurts like hell.

I'd just as soon go without as do it dry. You go in hard, the head jamming against the sides, and it feels just like sandpaper. You can't stop. He keeps right on pushing until you're sure you're going to suffocate. And spitting's no help. I heard about it once, but it's no good if you're a chicken. Chickens can't spit.

Usually there's no trouble, though. It hurts the geek, so he tries to keep it wet. Mine swallows castor oil before every show. Of course I come out greasy, but it's worth it. The feeling of being thrust through fully opened lips into a rose-colored damp, and down over a pink tongue into the tunnel of the throat! Ah! Its sides undulate against my feathers, sucking me into the welcome darkness, into the flaming pit of the stomach. God! The ecstasy!

My blood boils; my head pounds, I reach a peak, passion stiffens my limbs: and at that precise moment—he pulls me out. There I am, my entire being throbbing at a fever pitch of tension, and he stops. I'm left dangling by my feet… thwarted…frustrated…and *he* takes a goddamn bow. I hang upside down, suffering from cosmic blueballs, and he takes a bow.

But I can't leave it alone. Once you've had that glistening rosy wet skin caressing your body, you've got to have it: again and again.

So, there I was, act over, delirious with passion, and no way to let go. I hopped across the sand. Between the stakes there is enough of an opening to dart under, if you're small. Not that I'm kept caged. I'm free to roam wherever I want. And I do.

They're not afraid of losing me. I'm a very dependable chicken. None of that barnyard strain in me. I'm a circus pro. Even if I weren't, though, they couldn't miss me. Not with the color of my feathers. You see, when I got into this act, they dyed my feathers pink…*electro-magnetic* pink.

I stand out in a crowd. I hated it at first. I mean,

who ever heard of a pink chicken? But now that I've been this way for awhile, I kind of like it. I mean, you're not anonymous.

No. I didn't sneak out the back of the tent because I was running away or afraid of being caught. No siree...I went out the back because I would have been mobbed by autograph seekers if I had jumped off the stage after the act was over. My feathers would have been torn to shreds. Yes, to avoid hysterical fans this morning, I darted quietly out the back.

I scurried over to the tent of the fat lady. The Fair Rosamunda. Cautiously sliding past the limp canvas door, I went in. It was dark in the tent, and I couldn't see, but I heard panting and grunting from the other side. Finally my eyes adjusted. I turned one on them. I could make out two forms lying on a mattress. One was enormous and could be none other than the fat lady, but the other I couldn't figure out at all. Either it was very small, or it just seemed that way in contrast, but it was weird.

I hopped forward to get a better look and hid behind a pile of burlap bags. I could see the whole scene clearly, now. The figure on top was Quasimodo, the dwarf. They must have just started. The dwarf had been on stage only fifteen minutes ago. I was just in time. Whatever they were trying, it wasn't working.

Rosamunda was on her back, stark naked. Her breasts were the size of watermelons and lay drooping on her chest, falling over each arm. Her glistening stomach—they say she oils it—rolled mound after mound to a peak of quivering flesh.

My eyes ran down her blue-veined rump. This was going to be good. Quasimodo was stomach to stomach with her, balanced desperately to keep from falling to the floor. She must have picked him up bodily and put him there. Old Rosie is a hot one. She kept grunting and panting and grabbing for him, but he couldn't stay on her tummy.

"Sweetie, this isn't going to work," Quasimodo said. He slid to one side. To keep from falling any farther he grabbed a tit, holding on for dear life.

"Goddamn it. Stop yanking my boob. It hurts."

"My dear, if I weren't in mortal danger, I wouldn't be clutching your breast quite this way. Sometimes I feel that my yen for big women will be my downfall. We really have to find a different position. And even if I could stay on your delightful tum-tum, I doubt if I could satisfy either of us. You see, I can't reach my lady."

"It's okay, sweetie, we'll find something else. Where there's a will, there's a way," she screeched.

She threw both arms around him and sat up. Sweat rolled from her forehead to her cheeks, from her cheeks over the pimple by her mouth to the tip of her chin: it trickled over the edge of her second chin, past a bottomless crevice to her third chin and down the gentle slopes to her neck. It gushed into the crack between the gigantic mammaries, and dripped from her pubic hair. One delicate bead even dangled from her nipple for a while before dropping upon the nearest roll of her stomach.

She changed her position and ended up facing me. When she spread her legs, I nearly blew my top. There, between those white potato-shaped legs was a mouth that put my Geek's to shame. Sitting there, softly glistening in its own juices, deep and red, open and enticing, it was surrounded by tufts of kinky brown hair. My Geek had a mustache, too; but it was nothing like this.

There it was; a mouth meant to swallow. A bright pink tongue peeked out just a little from the sultry lips of this beautiful orifice. It made the blood roar through my veins, filling me with turgidity.

My god, what a hard-on.

Well, I barely had a chance to get settled before the damn dwarf sat down in front of her, blocking my view. Then the old bugger lay on his back, legs straight above him, feet on her chin. Then he stuck his cock in upside down! He pulled himself closer by grabbing her ass. Then he began pushing up and down, up and down, grunting and working up a lather. In and out, in and out, balls and cunt bouncing.

Humping. Humping is the word. It's much better than fucking. Hump makes the sweat and fat and funk of it more real.

He was grinding on his back, legs up straight. He gave it a run for his money, while Rosamunda chewed on his toes voraciously.

His body shook with the effort, driving itself in all directions, jerking faster and faster until the little fellow cried out, moaned, and became limp. I really thought he was dead, that the exertion had been too much for him. However after a few minutes he began to stir.

"Oh baby, you really know how to do it!" he gasped as he collapsed on the bed next to her.

His wet and shrinking prick flopped over on his left leg. The sound of his snoring drowned out her panting

Once more I was treated to the sight of her wet shiny orifice. The pressure in my cock pushed harder and tighter until it threatened to overflow. Pounding explosions, flashes of light, and a band playing Stars and Stripes Forever! I flapped over to the fat lady to pour my passion into that mouth…to dive head first into that great gushy opening…to be swallowed in its moist nirvana! Pointing, I did a cock point landing in her, softness against my hardness. It was too much! I threw my body against the great hairy hedge surrounding it. I heard a scream.

"Help! Get this fuckin' bird out of here! He's trying to fly up my ass!"

I half fell in my hurry to get away. Her voice was loud and I didn't want to be involved. The dwarf leapt up and began chasing me, swatting me with his trousers.

"Fucking pink chicken! I hope your Geek swallows you for good!"

I ducked as he swung those pants at my head. He was mean with a pair of pants. I flapped through the door and just missed being grabbed by the tail. I hopped through the dust to my own tent. I perched in what I hoped was an innocent spot and began cleaning the feathers between my legs. Outside I heard a voice.

"Fucking bird's a menace."

Someone else let out a coarse laugh.

"Old Fatty's had just about everything else, so why not a chicken?"

More laughter. My beak was burning! I didn't want everyone to know that I had lost control. This was one time when I definitely wished I weren't pink. I decided to be dignified about it, and continued cleaning my feathers. Anyway, they reeked! They stank like lox and musk.

I was standing on one foot cleaning my feathers,

laden with the fat lady's juices and my own, pulling them through my mouth to wipe them off, when the Geek walked in. I could see his legs and thighs. He pulled off his shirt, snorting as he crumpled it up, wiped the sweat from his face, and threw if in a basket. He kicked off his shoes, and went out.

He was gone for about five minutes, and he came back with a beer. He sat on a canvas stool, legs spread, and drank it. He guzzled half of it, then pulled down his zipper to give himself more room. From where I was perched I could see the bald spot at the top of his head and the sweat on his back soaking through his undershirt.

He was still drinking beer when Rosamunda burst in.

"You've *got* to do something about that damn chicken!"

"What's he done now?"

"He flew into my tent and attacked me. That's what!"

"Why'd he fly into your tent and attack you?"

"How the hell should I know? Because he's a menace, that's why!"

"What were you doing to him?"

"Nothing! I was sitting in my tent, minding my own business entertaining a friend, when this damn bird flapped at me!"

"How did you know it was my bird?"

17

"How many fucking pink chickens are there in this circus? It was your fucking chicken all right! I'd know it anywhere!"

"All right! All right already! So it's my bird. What'd he do to you? Did he hurt you?"

He wrapped his arm around the old girl, and began stroking the side of her neck, just under her ear. Then he kind of slid up close to her.

Well, there he was stroking her neck. Then he ran his hand down over her collarbone and began squeezing her tit. She started grinding hips, around and around, against his, and led like she was some kind of schoolgirl. He faced her and pulled the straps of her dress off her shoulders. It slid down her tits and over her stomach to a roll of fat somewhere between hips and belly button.

My Geek took one of her boobs in both hands. He pulled the hair around her nipple with his thumb, stroking the skin until the tip of her tan little tittie got hard and dark. Then he bent down and licked it with his tongue. The same tongue I tease and play with going down, and he used it to play with the fat lady's boob!

It kind of makes you sad that nothin's sacred these days. Then he put his mouth on it and started suckin', like he was gettin' a drink of milk or something. Maybe I'm too old-fashioned, but to see my Geek carrying on like that, with the fat lady, well it made my feathers ruffle! He was sucking and gettin' so loud that I thought the whole circus would hear. He pulled his mouth off and started kissing her on the stomach, grease and all.

His mouth slid down over the curves, and when he came to her belly button he poked it with his tongue, running around inside, licking up all the dust and lint. Rosamunda never washes her belly button. Then he got on his knees in front of her and grabbed her dress, pulling it down.

She stood still, a big lumpy hunk of woman, all shiny and naked. He tried to put his arms around her to grab her ass, but couldn't reach it, so he set her, stomach down, on a pile of dirty laundry. Then he pulled down his pants.

He was already hard, so he spread her legs and climbed on top. He shoved the cheeks of her ass open further, holding them as wide as he could, and damned if he didn't stick it in from the back! He got it all the way in and started pushing. And all the time fatty was moaning and twisting. She was breathing harder, beginning to pant and movin' her ass in circles, wrapping her legs around his, jerking faster and faster. My own cock, dangling in my feathers, had been getting harder and tighter and hotter. It really got to be a scorcher to stand and watch, so I started rubbing my prick against an orange crate, up and down, until I felt like I was going to drop from the effort, watching them screw like a downhill race or something. Then it all let go. The tension was gone...the spunk spurting out, I rubbed it all over the crate as it poured forth. I caught a splinter but I was feeling good. I looked down to see how the Geek and the fat lady were doing.

They were lying there with him still on top of her, and they were both panting and not saying a word. He pushed himself off and lay down next to her. She turned over and started tickling his stomach, running her hand down to his prick and grabbing it.

She ran her thumb and fingers along the top, squeezing the head and stroking it. Then she sat up and took his cock in her mouth, licking it, holding on like a little girl with a lollipop. She closed her eyes, smiled and pushed her mouth down onto it, pulling up and down on it with lips closed. My Geek's dick, which had been wilting, began to perk up, getting into the spirit of it as the fat lady sucked him off.

She pulled her lips up until just the head was in, still sucking, and he began to come, seed mixed with the spit that rolled out of her mouth.

Then she lay on her back and spread her own legs. The Geek sat up and pulled himself over the closest leg to lie on his stomach beside her, facing the cunt. He stuck his tongue way out and licked her hole with it. Then he ran his tongue inside, tickling the folds of skin at the tip, his nose half-buried in her pubic hair. His tongue reached in and darted farther into and out of her opening. She grabbed his head with both her hands and started yanking it hard against her cunt, moaning and twisting.

Well, the Geek started biting, really biting.

I could see his teeth from where I was roosting, and his jaws were clamping down. Smiling, she lay, legs twisted around him, moaning. Her hips moved faster and faster, slicked his mouth with juices and then she finally fell back limp, closed her eyes, and began to snore softly.

My Geek pushed away, stood up and walked over to his Listerine bottle, spitting the used mouthwash onto the floor. After he screwed the lid back on, he pulled up his pants, zipped them and went out.

About five minutes later he came back with another bottle of beer. Rosamunda woke up.

"Where am I?"

"You fell asleep," he said. "Would you like a beer?" he asked, handing her the bottle.

"No thanks...I've got to be going. I've got a date...."

"See you tomorrow."

"Yeah, good-bye. And don't forget to keep that chicken tied up."

"Yeah, sure. Have a good time."

"Don't I always?" she asked and went out laughing.

One thing about Rosamunda, she always managed to have a good time. I would have to be more careful from now on. I made a mental note to stay away from her for awhile. It was dark outside and way past my dinner time. I had worked up quite an appetite: sex always makes me hungry

I jumped down from my perch and began squawking to get his attention. I hopped over to the bag of hemp seeds he kept to feed me with, jumped up on it and began to crow. My Geek snickered.

"So, you're hungry are you, ya little bastard? You *should* be for all the trouble you got me into today. I shouldn't ought to feed you, but I suppose I'll have to or you'll drive me crazy."

Hemp of the evening, beautiful hemp.

My favorite seeds and he was giving them to me in fistful after fistful. I caught them, letting them roll into my gullet. If you ate enough, they would put you into the most cheerful mood and everything became hysterically funny. Beautiful shiny round nuggets. Sunshine pellets. I ate every one he threw down. I flapped up to the top of a pile of orange crates to let the seeds digest. The Geek went out to dinner with the rest of the circus and I fell asleep.

Chapter 2

I woke up as he returned. He tied the door behind him, pulling off his T-shirt as he walked across the sandy floor to the icebox. He opened it and took out a bowl of raspberry Jell-O. He set it out on the collapsible table and unzipped his pants. He grasped his limp prick and began jacking off until it grew hard. He picked up the bowl of Jell-O and held it close to his nuts, shoving it up so that the corona was skimming the surface. He rested it against the cold wet stuff for awhile, then stuck it in, breaking the surface, thrusting his cock into the Jell-O.

He drove his hips against the rim, the Jell-O slapping and churning. Chunks of Jell-O fell out. His hips jerked forward, and he panted and shook until he came, his own cream mixing with the Jell-O. He put the bowl on the table, reached for a spoon, sat down and ate the leftovers.

When he finished, he poured bottled water into it, and rinsed it out. From another box he pulled out a package of grape Jell-O, opened it, and poured the contents into the glass container. He poured some more water into a saucepan, and turned on the hot plate, putting the water on to boil. When it began bubbling, he poured a cup of it into the Jell-O powder and stirred it with his spoon until it dissolved. After it turned into a gummy liquid he added the same amount of cold water and put it in the icebox to set.

Then he put on a nightshirt, climbed into his sleeping bag, and went to sleep.

Chapter 3

"Hey! Someone get this fucking pink chicken out of here!"

"Whatsa matter in there, Charlie?"

"Can't even take a piss without that damn bird gawking! You'd think he gets his goodies that way!"

"He's a menace! You'd think the Geek would keep him locked up!"

"Probably hopin' he'll run away."

"Don't blame him. Fucking bird's a menace!"

"Heard he tried to fly up Rosie's cunt last night."

"I heard he made it!"

"I wouldn't be surprised. Old Rosie's had just about everything else, so why not a chicken?"

"Rosie's not bad. A little loose, but not bad."

"You had her too, Skychief?"

"Yeah, I had her."

"Damnation, that must have been some sight! How'd you do it? You're at least twice as tall as she is."

"Rosie's twice as fat, so it worked out."

"How'd you manage?"

"Simple. I leaned backwards off the side of the mattress and she placed her hot little cunt on my prick and rode like gangbusters. She's a real crusher. I nearly got gangrene!"

"Was the chicken watching?"

"If I caught any chicken watching me fuck, that chicken would be stew before he knew what hit him!"

"That's what Rosie said."

"I've got longer legs."

"You sure do. I hear people talk and they say you use stilts for your act."

"The hell I do! Hey Charlie, throw me the soap."

"Here. You know, I bet it was kind of funny... that stupid bird flappin' at Rosie like he's going to dive down her cunt."

"She'd never feel it!"

"Ha! Ha!"

"Shit! There's that fucking chicken again! Catch him!"

"Corner him!"

"I'll get him from over here!"

"Get him! He's getting away!"

"Block the door!"

"Grab him! Grab him!"

"Chicken stew tonight!"

"Not if he gets away! Grab him!"

Chapter 4

I seem to be encountering a great deal of hostility lately.

My unfortunate affair with the fat lady seems to have put them on their guard. It's harder to watch unnoticed these days. Perhaps if my Geek would change my feather color....

I just can't seem to avoid Rosamunda. Earlier, out of boredom, I hopped over to the lion cage where the tame lion for the cat act lived. The tamer was there when I arrived and was throwing chunks of raw meat to his pet.

Up close, the lion's roar was deafening. I perched out of sight on the metal hook used to connect this wagon to the others when we were on the road. Just as he was bending down to pick up a hunk of bloody meat, Rosamunda waddled around the corner of the cage, squeezed into a silk, skin tight orange dress. Its neckline plunged deep into her cleavage and was hidden by two white carnations.

"Can I help?" she purred, stroking his ear.

"Yeah, if you can wait until I feed the cat."

"Sure. Careful of the blood!"

She sat down on the grass, resting on one hip, and pulled down the strap to her dress, exposing a shoulder. She looked at him out of the corner of her eye, giving him that "come-on" smile. She began wiggling her ass and pulled the carnations away from her boobs so he could see her. He walked over and pinched her tit.

"I've got a fuck that you'll never forget, baby."

Rosie gurgled and reached for him.

"Lay on your back, doll, and pull up your dress."

Her legs were spread just enough to give me a peek at that delicious mouth. There it was, still wet and shiny. I could smell the lovely smoked salmon odor of her cunt! I took a deep breath and stayed where I was. The lion tamer reached down between her legs and stuck his fingers in her vagina. He wiggled them around.

"You're ready. Now turn over and get on your hands and knees."

He pulled her skirt up further on her. Her great lumpy rump gleamed in the sunshine. From where I was, the view was beautiful. Peeping through the brown hair growing between her legs, was a slip of pink, and the tip of her clit.

"I'm going to blindfold you."

"Blindfold me? What for?"

"You'll like it better that way. It's part of the act."

"Well, okay."

So he put a blindfold around her, then went over to the lion's cage and led it out. The lion spotted Rosie, his cock began to swell, so he leaped on her and mounted her. He shoved his prick in hard and started fucking her, clawing the air and roaring. No one was paying any attention, so I hopped over to the cage to get a better look, and started getting excited myself. It really got tight, the blood pressure building. I couldn't help rubbing myself against the bar of the cage. Meanwhile poor Rosie had discovered that it was a lion.

"You son of a bitch! Whatsa big idea siccing your fucking cat on me? Everybody said you were queer!"

"All I promised, my dear, was an unforgettable fuck. He won't hurt you—he's declawed and you could always roll over on top of him and crush him."

"Up yours! Just wait until I get at you, ya schmuck! Your cream will be curdled from here to kingdom come! You and your cat both!"

Poor Rosie was scared shitless to pull away the cat before he was finished so she just stayed on her hands and knees, hating it. She tore the blindfold off, to give the trainer a dirty look and was still glaring at him when the lion came.

I had managed to relieve myself on the bars of the lion cage. The lion pulled himself off, and bounced back into the cage. Unfortunately, I was still in it. He let out a roar when he saw me and jumped. He'd had dinner and didn't put much effort into it, but his roar drew the attention of the tamer. By squawking and crowing and flapping my wings, I was able to hold him off. I managed to get out before the tamer slammed the cage door.

"Fucking chicken! The next time you won't be so lucky!"

A rock hurled through the air landed beside me. I flapped to give myself a higher ground speed, and got the hell away! Another stone landed in front. I took an instant dislike to the lion tamer.

Finally I was out of range and hopped into the brightly colored tent of the acrobatic team. The radio was tuned to a longhair station, and they were making love in time to a Mozart concerto.

Rocco was standing, legs apart, holding onto the

legs of Giovanni. Giovanni's legs were wrapped around the waist of Rocco, his feet, sole to sole, against Rocco's stomach. Giovanni had his prick buried deep in the muscular rump of his brother, while his own body was arched backwards, head nearly touching the floor, hands around Rocco's ankles. Then, all in time to the slow piano he let go of Rocco's ankles and straightened his back. Then he pulled himself up slowly until he could wrap his arms around Rocco's neck. Then Rocco slowly somersaulted so that Giovanni was lying on his back on the floor, with Rocco on top. All this time Giovanni never took his cock out once!

They began rocking back and forth, still in time to the music until Giovanni cried out, and shaking his cock, he collapsed and sat very still.

Rocco rolled off him, got up and dressed. Pretty soon, Giovanni got dressed too, and they both went out. I couldn't believe that performance! So that's how they keep in practice!

Aren't they lucky chickens can't talk?

I noticed voices outside the tent, and the sound of many shoes on hard-packed dust. I decided it must be close to showtime. I had an act to do, so I hopped back to my Geek's tent to get ready.

Chapter 5

STEP RIGHT UP FOLKS AND SEE THE WONDROUS MAGIC
SHOW...THE FATTEST LADY IN THE WORLD...THE FAIR
ROSAMUNDA! SEE IGOR, THE REPTILE MAN, COVERED
WITH SCALES...YES, YOU HAVE TO SEE IT TO BELIEVE IT!
STEP RIGHT UP AND SEE THE SNAKE CHARMER CHARM
HIS POISONOUS AND DEADLY SNAKES...THE KING
COBRA...THE MYSTIC ANACONDA! STEP RIGHT UP
FOLKS...STEP RIGHT UP AND WATCH NICK THE GEEK
ATTEMPT THE IMPOSSIBLE...AND SUCCEED...HE SWAL-
LOWS THINGS THAT WOULD KILL AN ORDINARY
MORTAL...AND YET HE LIVES...WATCH HIM SWALLOW A

YO-YO! WATCH HIM SWALLOW A SWORD COVERED WITH FLAME! WATCH HIM SWALLOW A LIVE CHICKEN FIGHTING FOR ITS LIFE AS IT GOES DOWN! AH, YES FOLKS...STEP RIGHT UP AND SEE THE SHOW. ONLY FIFTY CENTS WILL SHOW YOU THE AMAZING BEARDED LADY AND NOT ONLY THAT BUT THE WORLD'S TALLEST MAN...AND LAST BUT NOT LEAST...THE DWARF MAN! THIS WAY FOLKS...THIS WAY...JUST PAY THE LADY IN THE BOOTH AND WALK RIGHT IN!

"You're on Nick! Hurry it up!"

"Yeah, yeah, I know. I'm coming. I'm just getting my stuff. Help me catch the chicken."

AND HERE HE IS FOLKS, NICHOLAS, THE GEEK! THERE HE IS FOLKS...A KING SIZED YO-YO...RIGHT DOWN THE HATCH...WATCH HIS THROAT...THERE IT IS FOLKS. OUT AGAIN...THERE HE GOES FOLKS...HE JUST DIPPED THE SWORD IN KEROSENE! WATCH HIM SET IT ON FIRE! HE IS GOING TO PUSH IT, FLAMES AND ALL, DOWN HIS THROAT...THERE IT GOES! THE FLAMING BLADE IS DOWN HIS THROAT! THE PAIN, FOLKS...CAN YOU IMAGINE THE PAIN? THOSE FLAMES ARE REAL! REAL FLAMES AND HE'S SWALLOWING THEM! YES FOLKS...THERE HE GOES...THE SWORD IS OUT AND STILL FLAMING AND THE MAN IS STILL ALIVE! AH, YES. STRANGE THINGS IN THIS WORLD...WHAT COULD BE STRANGER THAN LIFE? BUT WAIT—THAT'S NOT ALL...NO SIRREE...THE ACT HAS JUST

BEGUN! SEE THAT CHICKEN? THE PINK ONE? HE'S GOING TO SWALLOW IT...RIGHT DOWN HIS THROAT...FULL OF LIFE...KICKING AND FIGHTING...SEE THAT FOLKS.

THE BIRD IS FIGHTING! HE'S RISKING LIFE AND LIMB TO SWALLOW THAT CHICKEN! THERE HE GOES...CRAMMING THAT BIRD DOWN HIS THROAT! WATCH HIM! THE BIRD HAS COMPLETELY DISAPPEARED! HE'S PULLING IT OUT NOW. SEE THE CHICKEN'S LEGS...SEE HIS HEAD. WADDYA KNOW FOLKS! A WORLD WONDER THAT REALLY DESERVES YOUR APPLAUSE! TAKE A BOW NICK! A HAND FOR THE CHICKEN ON THE WAY OUT!

A flaming sword is a tough act to follow.

Chapter 6

So there I was, primed with excitement, glistening
with castor oil, pinfeathers prickling. I made my
way over to the snake charmer's, a place I usually
avoid. I can't stand snakes. They scare me shitless,
and if I'd been in a sharper frame of mind, I would
have avoided it today. But I didn't. I hopped
through the flap and perched behind a grass
basket. The charmer was sitting cross-legged on
the floor, smoking a hand-made cigarette, staring
outside. He was still in costume with a white
diaper and a turban wrapped around his head. I

hadn't been there long when to my surprise, in walked the Reptile Man. He was completely covered with greenish scales. And wore a leather cape, boots, and a black leather jockstrap. He strode up to the charmer, swinging his cape, and stood before him, arms folded.

"Stand up!"

The charmer stood, head bowed.

"Where is the snake?"

The little man pointed to a grass basket over in the far corner of his tent.

"Bring it to me!"

The swami scurried across the tent to the basket, leathery feet kicking up puffs of dust He lifted the rattan container to waist level, and, sweating under the strain, carried it to his scaly master. He set it down gingerly in front of the Reptile Man and stood before him, waiting. Reptile Man took the lid off and laid it on the floor beside the basket and reached in, pulling out a boa constrictor. The snake wrapped itself around the shingled arm, squeezing in reflex action. Glowering at the meek figure in front of him, Reptile Man ordered:

"Take your clothes off."

The snake charmer snapped open the safety-pin fastening the cloth around him, and taking the end in one hand, began very slowly to unwind the gauzy diaper. He pulled it from around his loins once, then again, then a third time, until he had the yardage partially in his hands and partially between his legs, wrapped around his thighs, still hiding the shaft and head of his dubious manhood. He drew it under his legs, then unwound it from around his other leg to stand completely exposed, the yellow-stained cloth trailing from his clenched fist. He stood, in liver-spotted nakedness, head bowed before the Reptile Man, his shriveled testicles dangling dismally between his legs.

"On your knees!"

The Reptile Man pulled the snake from his arm by brute strength, twirling it around him, holding tightly to it just below the head. I could hear the air hiss as it whirled and a screaming smack as the snake was lashed heavily down onto the swami's bony back, forcing a harsh moan out of him as the pain grabbed at his diaphragm and stomach muscles. His face turned purple as the tears rolled from his eyes, and his body shook as the snake-whip lashed down a second time, across his bare buttocks. As the giant reptile slashed into his ass, again and again, leaving huge red welts, his prick stiffened. With each new gash on his body, the shaft became straighter and harder until it stood at attention. The streaks on his flesh were raw as the snake was brought down on his shrunken body, and as they began to bleed, a thick white liquid spewed from his cock.

The snake wasn't too pleased and his mouth was open like he wanted to swallow the both of them.

I was ready to duck under the tent and get the hell out before the boa spotted me. Boas eat chickens and I'm not about to get swallowed permanently.

But then my Geek walked in.

"Darling!" he said to the Reptile Man and started pulling off his pants. He was already hard, and grabbed the Reptile Man from behind and stuck his prick up the scaly rear. He threw his arms around the Reptile Man's hips and grabbed his balls. He commenced jacking him off from behind.

While my Geek was jacking the Reptile Man, the little snake charmer was still getting his from the snake, moaning and twisting like he was really loving it. In the meantime, the snake was fighting back and getting more and more hysterical; he doubled up on himself and wrapped his body around the necks of the Reptile Man and my Geek, and started squeezing. I was cheering for my Geek, of course, but at the same time I couldn't blame the snake very much either. My Geek grabbed the loose end and pulled him off the Reptile Man. Pretty soon they had it under control and back in its basket.

I knew that snake was pissed and that basket lid didn't look too secure, so I ducked out. I squeezed under the bottom and went hopping toward the main tent. A few people were wandering around, there to see the next show, and a little girl threw me some popcorn.

I really don't like popcorn, but when you get it for free, you can't complain.

Chapter 7

"Oh Mommy! A pink chicken! Can I have him? Huh? Huh?"

"Of course you can't have him!"

"But I want him! Oh please mommy lemme have the pink chicken! I wanna pink chicken! Lemme have the pink chicken!"

"Shut up! You're *not* getting no pink chicken and that's final!"

"I am too! I wanna pink chicken! I hate you! You're a mean old lady! I wanna *chicken! Oh please* lemme have the pink chicken!"

"If you don't shut up, we're going home!"

"But I wanna pink chicken!"

"I don't want no chickens hanging around the house crapping up the furniture and that's final! You're *not* getting no pink chickens! Now get back here!"

"C'mere chicken!"

He ran toward me.

"Lemme play with you!"

I flapped like hell to get away. This kid didn't look good and he was fast. I thoroughly agreed with Mommy, and didn't want to hang around her house, playing with that kid. I moved!

"Oh please Chickey, I wanna play with you!" Well I didn't want to play with *him!* Up ahead I saw the horse for the bareback act. I flapped onto a pile of boxes, and from there to safety on his back. Unfortunately the rather excitable Arabian steed became upset at my expected appearance on him, and bolted.

Lurching forward, he galloped, crashing into crates housing the trained pig act, freeing ten hysterically squealing head of pork into the crowd.

An old lady screamed as two pigs thrashed toward her, hurling her into the crowd, wheelchair in third gear. Others saw the loosed animals, panicked and ran in all directions.

I jumped off and hopped for cover before anyone

could notice me, and watched the whole thing from behind a large pile of manure.

Finally, one of the trainers caught the horse and led him to the main tent, the horse snorting indignantly and shaking the sweat from his body.

Catching the pigs was another matter. They were fast and enjoyed their freedom. One of the crew would make a flying tackle to grab one, only to find it had slipped out of his arms. By show time he had managed to get all but one.

I heard the band signaling the beginning of the show.

Chapter 8

What a day! I thought I had troubles before. What a laugh! They were nothing compared to what happened today.

Early this morning I was wandering around the circus, bored silly, with a couple of hours to kill until the first show. A few people were up, like Rocco, who was doing ballet exercises behind his tent. Further on, one of the clowns was washing his underwear.

Past them, I saw the ringmaster's wife standing in a patch of dew-dampened crab grass, slipping her hand under the waistband of her skirt. Reaching deep she fingered her pussy. The material covering the crotch bounced as her hand thrust into the cavern, stroking the plump flesh with her thumb. She looked bored and slouched as her fingers worked, only her hips twitching in response.

She was staring at the sky and looking faintly disgusted when the ringmaster himself walked out, gleaming in nakedness. He saw what she was doing and scowled.

"Playing with yourself again! That's all you ever do...play with yourself. Why?"

"Because I like to play with myself," she sneered. "It feels good!"

"Now listen here..." he began. His face became livid. Drawing himself up to his full height of four feet five inches, he strutted in a circle around her.

"I demand an explanation! A man has the right to know why his wife plays with herself, doesn't he?"

Flippantly she slapped his little pink prick with the back of her hand.

"That's why," she sniggered, her hand still pumping her cunt.

"What's wrong with it? It works fine. It gets me to the bathroom without a hitch. What do you have to complain about?"

"Nothing," she said sweetly, smiling. "I happen to like my finger better, that's all."

She turned away and continued, doggedly, to masturbate. Turning even more livid as he watched, his eyes changed from impotent anger to crafty determination. With one swift movement, he grabbed his prick and aimed it, letting loose a yellow jet of water to drench the back of her skirt. She gasped and lunged at him, screaming.

"Why you dirty son of a bitch! Of all the fucking nerve…pissing on my skirt! I'll have your head on a platter for that! You just wait 'til I get through with you!"

"We get what we pay for in this life," he yelled running into the tent. She followed, shaking her fist.

"What the hell is that supposed to mean? Worm! Come back here, you!"

He ran around the outside to the back again, pulling a flowered nightshirt over his stomach to cover the offending parts. His angry wife followed close, bare boobies bouncing in the soft glow of morning, the back of her skirt shimmering wetly. He ducked into the tent again, wife hot on his heels. Inside were muffled voices.

"What the fuck am I gonna wear now? Answer me that, you little worm? It was my only clean skirt!" Metal crashed against metal.

"Wear a *dirty* skirt. I don't know!"

A sauce pan sailed through the door and over my

head to land in the wet grass behind me. Inside, breaking glassware drowned out their shouting. A coffee cup whirled over me and crashed into a tree, scattering shrapnel in all directions.

It was getting dangerous so I decided to be on my way, leaving them to wedded bliss.

I waddled on, not stopping until I came to the pink and blue tent of the hermaphrodite. As I stood near the opening, I heard voices. Consumed by curiosity, I squeezed under the bottom. Due to the extremely small space, I was forced to scrape my breast on the gravel-littered ground. I would have to watch my weight from now on.

Once inside, I was hidden by a pile of ostrich feathers. It was part of the hermaphrodite's costume, a tasty contraption involving a glitter-covered breastplate worn under a gauzy over-blouse on the SHE side, and half of a matching satin Cossack shirt on the HE side. The bottom of the costume was a trouser leg sewn to a short feather skirt, and net stockings.

Actually the indecisive creature wasn't put together half and half down the middle but the circus is a place of hallowed tradition. The marks expect it. If they knew anything about hermaphrodites, they would realize that a neat division is impossible.

Our hermaphrodite, for instance, had a woman's

bone structure, narrow-waisted with small shoulders. The arms were jointed like a female, with an outward angle from the elbow down. The hips sloped from the waist to form luscious rounded thighs and shapely legs.

Until today I couldn't be sure it was thing more than a fem-type male. Since the truth was unfortunately hidden under the pants-skirt, I had never seen the telltale features.

As I peered through the wispy feathers, hermaphrodite tugged a powder blue nightgown over its head to reveal the moist lips of a cunt, hairless, its inner folds glisteningly pink, and just like anybody else's cunt except for the sperm sac hanging beneath, serving a small penis that sprouted from inside the mouth-like opening.

In the shadows behind the hermaphrodite crouched Moxie the Bearded Lady, stroking the hair of her face as she eyed her friend. She was naked. The hair covering her chest extended over her tuberous mammaries to thin out near the hairless nipples. Her stomach was smooth except for one tuft of hair sprouting out of her belly button. Kinky hair grew from her hips and ran down her legs. Her pubic region was smooth and grew pink as her fingers stroked its plumpness.

"Come here, Hermes," she addressed the hermaphrodite.

He slouched, stared at the floor, not daring to move.

"Hermes!" she said. "*Dear sweet* Hermes, are you going to force me to *seduce* you?"

Hermes shrugged and continued to study the floor.

"Hermes, virginity is not good for you. Think of your health."

Hermes giggled, refusing to look at her.

"Sit down, Hermes. Next to me."

The lad, or lass—depending on your preference—slowly shuffled to the bearded lady, bent knees and slowly sank to the dust beside her.

"Relax, Hermes. It won't hurt."

The undecided creature sat, resigned to what fate she had in store.

"That's better. Actually you're quite fortunate. You can enjoy the pleasures of both sexes. That's a one in a million talent. Now lie back," she said briskly.

Hermes meekly obeyed. She reached for the limp prick. Taking it in her hand, she stroked the head with her thumb, kneading the yielding flesh with a sure motion. With the fingers of her other hand she reached deep into the slickness of his female parts and explored the hidden recesses, tickling the warm shaft surrounding its penis. Hermes moaned as the soft prick raised itself by degrees to a full erection, catching, as it stiffened, the juice dribbling out of the cunt.

Moxie climbed on him, her open mouth hovering over the prick. The lips of her cunt touched the lips of his mouth in glorious sexual union. She clamped her jaws on the virginal cock, sucked it with the strong muscles of her cheeks, delicately running her tongue down the shaft. She lifted her mouth from it, then taking the testicles in her cupped hands she bent down to them, sucking heavily. She withdrew to leave an angry purple passion mark on the tender flesh.

As Hermes lay panting with sweat pouring down his face, she nipped the cockhead that was imprisoned between her teeth.

"Tongue me," the infamous bearded lady ordered.

"Tongue you?" replied Hermes in bewilderment.

"Shit, are you dumb! Do you think I have my cunt up to your face for nothing? Stick your tongue into my slit, push it in and out, stir it around and make me come. Use your teeth if you want. I like it rough."

Hermes gingerly poked into her opening and awkwardly stabbed. Darting into her, the tongue pulled away with reptilian speed, and hid inside the lips of its owner.

"Harder! Don't just poke. Get your mouth in there and *dig!*"

Hermes leaned forward on his elbow to cover her cunt completely with an open mouth. Dutifully, jaw working up and down, the teeth dug into the hairless flesh, ever harder, to chew with strong primary incisors. From the stretched throat muscles I could tell that Hermes was pushing the tongue deep into her vagina and probing.

Licking.

Tasting.

From the facial expression worn, I could tell that he, she, or whatever, had serious doubts about the whole sex thing.

Slowly, as Moxie sucked, the hermaphrodite got into the spirit and gleefully nipped at her clit.

Hard.

"Ouch! That hurts!" she squawked. "Would you like it if I bit your balls that way?"

"Feels good," Hermes answered vaguely.

"Oh, no it doesn't, so stop it."

Hermes bit the tip of her clit again.

"I told you to lay off my clit with your goddamn teeth! Now you asked for it." She snarled and bit the testicles.

"Ah ah ah ah!" wailed the half-man, writhing in agony.

Moxie, being somewhat of a sadist, gnawed the tender flesh of the scrotum with her front teeth.

Hermes, being somewhat of a masochist,

groaned, writhing as the white fluid spurted out of his penis to drip off the tip onto the lady's beard.

"Oh nuts!" bitched Moxie. "I get all the goodies! I shoulda known anyone as freaky as you would like pain. Now I gotta shampoo my beard."

She stood and walked to her overnight bag.

"I got something else for you," she said, pulling a leather dildo from the bulbous sack. "You have had one male experience. Now you're gonna get fucked."

She strapped the ersatz prick to her loins, fastening the buckle at one side as she sauntered toward him.

"This might hurt. I'm gonna pop your cherry if you have a cherry to pop. You might not, you know. You're pretty freaky."

"You keep reminding me."

"I'm sorry, kid," she said comfortingly. "Now just relax and spread your legs. The more you relax, the less it'll hurt."

Hermes obeyed, lying tense while she carefully rubbed her instrument with Vaseline Petroleum Jelly, smearing an extra heavy coat on the head. She knelt and shoved her fingers into his vagina. After satisfying herself that he was properly lubricated, she straddled him, and inserted the head of her "penis" into the folds of his cunt. She stroked the inner edges, gently thrusting deeper and deeper. With her final thrust he cried out in pain, and blood dripped from the opening, flowing out of the wound onto the prick to drip off the head onto the sand.

Hermes' loins contracted, pushing upward to hers in even four/four rhythm. Frantically, as sweat poured, his muscles worked in unison with hers, sharing the agony of climax.

Collapsed, a vapid grin spread on the face of the hermaphrodite, eyes glazing as he giggled hysterically.

Moxie rolled off his body and landed on her back. She twisted and unfastened the dripping dildo, flinging it at her overnight bag. It landed in the sand.

"Aren't you going to wash it off?" asked Hermes, obviously an anal-retentive freako for tidiness.

"I'll do it later," replied Moxie.

"Do it now, please. I can't stand the way it looks. Besides it'll be harder to clean later. All that grit will harden and you'll have to use steel wool. That would ruin the surface and I can hardly see you sending it out to be dry cleaned."

"All right! All right! For Crissake!" wailed Moxie in annoyance as she pushed herself off the ground. "What am I going to wash it off with?"

"I haven't poured out the dishwater yet. It's over near the hot plate," said Hermes, pointing to it.

As Moxie dunked the used dildo into the soapsuds, scrubbing it with her host's dish cloth, I noticed that the hermaphrodite was hard again.

"Come here!" said Hermes.

Moxie turned and stared at his prick.

"You're learning fast," she said approvingly.

She lay on her back at his side waiting expectantly to be fucked. Hermes, of course, fucked her.

After that was done, Hermes (being new to sex) decided to experiment. Prick in hand, he bent it up and stuck it into his own cunt. Partially erect, the experiment was successful, but as it pushed, the friction from prick against cunt forced a full erection which in turn had the unfortunate effect of forcing the penis out and away from his vagina, thereby making intercourse with himself impossible. I decided that if Hermes had the self-discipline to maintain a partial erection, he could while away many happy hours.

Chapter 9

I heard voices outside and realized that I had forgotten to keep track of the time. Sticking my head out a hole I saw people milling around. Parents dragging children sticky from cotton candy, teenagers in beads and sandals, and elderly people hobbling on canes, all directed by off-duty policemen in uniform. It was show time and I was late.

I dragged my ass from the hermaphrodite's tent and hurried to the sideshow tent. The Geek, red-faced, was pacing the floor and muttering to himself. He spotted me as I approached and roared.

"Fucking chicken, where the hell you been? I ought to wring your neck. I'll serve you in chicken soup! You're more trouble than you're worth."

He grabbed me by the legs, but I tried to hop away. I squawked, trying to make him realize he was hurting me.

"Hey Nick! I see you found the bird."

"Yeah, the son of a bitch wandered in just now. Thanks to him I had to let Rosie go on ahead of me. The barker is probably pissed like hell, announcing me and getting Rosie. Pain in the ass! I should keep him tied up."

"A hell of a fighter, isn't he?"

Well, of course I was! The Geek hurt me, dangling me upside down and squeezing my legs. Worse, I was horny from watching the scene in the hermaphrodite's tent, and had, to my dismay, a full erection. Naturally I had doubts about being swallowed in that condition and managed to get rid of it before I did my act.

"Nick, if I was you, I'd put him in a cage. He's pretty wild today. He could fly off and leave you with just your sword and yo-yo."

Well, of course I wasn't going to run off! The nerve of that bum. All I wanted was a quiet corner somewhere to jack off in peace.

"You're probably right, Joe. Hand me that crate."

So there I was, penned up like any common barnyard fowl. I felt definitely claustrophobic. Trying to make the best of a bad situation, I rubbed my prick against the wooden slats of my prison, but alas, it didn't work. Still throbbing, the flesh rising between my legs demanded release. Getting none, it stubbornly resisted any attempts to hoodwink it into softening, and remained where it was, jutting from my feathers.

Someone lifted the crate high and carried it onto the stage. I heard applause, laughter.

"Hey Nick," someone near whispered. "I see you caught the little motherfucker."

"Yeah. Thought I'd have to find a new chicken."

"Be better off if you did."

"Tell you what," said the Geek. "A dollar fifty and he's yours. He'd make a good fryer. A dollar fifty buys you Sunday dinner."

"Hell no!" said the other. "I got troubles of my own. Listen to him carry on. You'd almost think he understands what we were saying."

"Nah. Too dumb. You heard the term 'birdbrain'? They invented it for him."

Well! *Me* a "birdbrain"! I squawked my indignation to the skies and told *them* a thing or two. A pity they were too dumb to understand. I would have blasted them to the moon. And good riddance!

The crowd was jolted. Peering out I could see the audience waiting for the Geek to begin his act.

YES HERE IT IS FOLKS, THE ACT YOU'VE BEEN WAITING FOR...NICHOLAS THE GEEK!

(Where the hell you been anyway?)

YES SIRREE FOLKS, YOU ARE ABOUT TO WITNESS THE IMPOSSIBLE...RIGHT BEFORE YOUR VERY EYES!

(You better make it good...they were pissed when Rosie showed instead of you. Wish you could of told me sooner...)

THERE HE GOES FOLKS...DOWN THE HATCH! LOOK AT THAT! THE YO-YO DOWN HIS THROAT AND UP AGAIN WITHOUT A HITCH! NOW I DON'T WANT NONE OF YOU KIDDIES OUT THERE TRYING THAT...YA HEAR? IT'S DANGEROUS! WILLYA LOOK AT THAT FOLKS...DID IT WITHOUT EVEN TRYING! HOW ABOUT THAT!

(Whatsa matter with the chicken Nick? What's he crated up for?)

"Been acting strange."

"Trouble? Gonna use him?"

"Thought I'd try."

"Lotsa luck."

"Thanks."

YES FOLKS THOSE ARE REAL FLAMES HE'S TAKING INTO HIS THROAT...HE'S CRAMMING A REAL SWORD! THE PAIN! THINK OF THE PAIN FOLKS! THAT FIRE MAKIN' A BARBECUE OUTA THE INSIDE OF HIS THROAT! HURTS TO

WATCH DOESN'T IT? HE'S STILL ALIVE! HE PULLED THE SWORD OUT, AND HE'S STILL STANDING ON HIS OWN FEET! AND NOW FOLKS…THE CROWNING EVENT! MOST AMAZING OF ALL THAT MAN'S GONNA SWALLOW A *LIVE CHICKEN!* ALIVE AND KICKING, CLAWING TO GET AWAY AND OUR MAN'S GONNA TAKE AND PUT IT DOWN HIS THROAT!

At that, the Geek pulled me out upside down and held me tight. Well, I mean to tell you I was flapping! I meant business. I had to get away and rid myself of that damned hard-on, but he wouldn't let me go. Grinning faces, upside down, stared at me and waited.

Leering. I wondered if they could see it. I suppose I shouldn't have been embarrassed. Monkeys get hard-ons all the time. They never feel embarrassed, so why should I? After all, monkeys are higher on the scale of evolution anyway.

I dropped helplessly toward the cavern below.

It loomed closer, growing inch by inch. Those lips, the entranceway into the body. The tongue, flattened and exposed was coated with thick white scum. It was to pad my landing. Into the tunnel, scraping past the jagged white fang teeth, sinking deeper, watching as I sank into the growing darkness. In the airless black I waited as usual. For light, for breath, to be pulled back in one orgasmic catharsis of freedom to face daylight and boring applause.

But today it didn't happen quite that way. On the way down, my hardened prick had gotten caught in the Geek's throat, stuck in the space behind the uvula and the section in front where the uvula dangles. Well, to make a long story short, I got it stuck behind that second flap of skin and the Geek couldn't get me out!

He panicked and yanked at me again and again, causing my prick to rub against his throat. This forced the loose skin up and down in rhythm, beating me off inside him. I had practically suffocated when the jacking off motion finally freed the stoked-up come, letting it roll down the Geek's throat. The stuff spilled down the back of his esophagus to mix with his stomach acid. I thought of my spermatozoa rushing through his bloodstream to nourish his cells, the rest issuing through as waste and out to freedom, fertilizing some other organism to grow and live anew in other forms. Thoughts of the complete death and life cycle churned in my brain, too long cut off from oxygen.

With a swish of movement, flashing daylight.

Dark forms, clapping hands, cheered me as I hung limp, drunken with success. The Geek held me high.

Much to my chagrin, his face was purple and he seemed upset about something. I couldn't understand this in the light of the applause we were receiving. I, for one, was gratified that the audience had finally learned to appreciate my performance.

As for the prick that had caused all this excitement, it was hanging comfortably and at peace. I felt good and when the Geek freed me, I hopped back to his tent for a good snooze.

Chapter 10

"Oh Maudie, wasn't that the living end? The way the wonderful man nearly suffocated with that chicken down his throat?"

"Don't be naive, Esther. It was a trick. They do it to make you think they're in danger, but they're not. It's part of the act."

"It looked real to me. His face turned purple. I saw it."

"It's a trick they do with makeup. It's timed to change color at a certain time. You can work miracles with Max Factor these days."

"How do you know what brand it was? Do they carry a line of makeup timed to go off at a certain time?"

"No, no. It's just a figure of speech. I could have said Revlon or Coty, but I didn't, I said Max Factor. I just happened to think of it first, that's all. I don't know *what* company puts out makeup like that chicken swallower wore. Actually it's probably some weird brand that only circus people and actors know about."

"Oh. Well, it was still a good show. Had *me* fooled."

"Of course it was a good show. That's what they're getting paid for isn't it? At fifty cents it *ought* to be a good show. But don't let it fool you, honey. It's no different than when a trapeze performer has a near miss."

"Yeah, I suppose so."

"Oh look! There's the chicken!"

"Where?"

"Up there. On that pile of boxes. How can you miss him? He's so pink."

"I'm color-blind."

"Well over there, right where I'm pointing! You see?"

"Oh yeah, I see him now. Funny-looking, isn't he?"

"Probably a special circus breed."

"It's funny how they let him run free like that. You'd think they'd be afraid he'd run away."

"Chickens are a dime a dozen."

Well, a hell of a lot *she* knew! What a blowhard! "Chickens are a dime a dozen." Bullshit is alive and well in the circus. Maybe barnyard stock, but certainly not a trained specialist like me. And that theory about timed makeup! Egad, what a pile of shit! I've heard of makeup turning orange on certain skin types, but it was a haphazard thing. If makeup companies could time makeup to change color, it would be a major breakthrough. Of course it would be a problem since there is really no use for it, but if they had it they could think up something for it. They could promote eyeshadow that turned from green to silver at five P.M. It would be for women who had a heavy date right after they left the office. Or they could perfect a base that changed from natural to brown for those who wanted to go slumming in Harlem after they spent a few hours at their White Anglo-Saxon Protestant country club. Of course that could cause problems too. They'd have to leave before it started changing or they might risk being blackballed by their clubmates for being secret Negroes. It could blow the whole white supremacy image. But if they remembered to wear a watch they would have no such problem. Actually, come to think of it, timed makeup wasn't such a bad idea after all.

Still I was pissed at the old girl for making those remarks about my looks. Like who did she think she was, anyway, Raquel Welch? If I had a face like hers I'd bury it in the sand, or subsidize a plastic surgeon.

Chapter 11

Well, after I left the old biddy giggling at my funny looks and pink feathers, I went back to the Geek's tent to freshen before dinner. I had a raging appetite. Unfortunately, I couldn't do much about it until he got back.

You see, a few days ago I had gotten hungry and broke into the feed sack. It's not easy for a chicken to maneuver, and I somehow managed to spill a great deal of seed onto the floor. Well, the Geek bitched, ranting about the price of hemp on the open market and all that. From then on, he tied the top of the bag with wire. Try as I might, I haven't been able to open it since. I was hopping around on one foot impatiently, when the Geek finally got back. I clucked loudly to get his attention, and jumped over to the feed sack to remind him that it was my dinner hour. He absently opened it and threw a few handfuls on the floor. He tied the bag again, then sat in his canvas chair, staring into space.

After I had devoured most of it, settling down to roost, I was distracted by the appearance of Tom the Trapeze Boy and his ten-year-old sister Consuela.

"Señor Nicholas, I heard about your most awful accident from one of the other acrobats. Is it true? Did you really approach death this afternoon?"

"I came close."

"How did it happen?"

"I don't know. The chicken got stuck in my throat and I couldn't pull it out. I really don't know."

Well, I knew! I also knew that if I had any choice, the Geek wasn't going to know. If he found out, it would be curtains. No more hemp seed, no more circus, no more sex.

Visions of chicken soup floated through my head. Me looking out from inside, my feathers plucked, shamelessly naked, being dunked head first into a pot of boiling water, to simmer for about five hours, was a particularly disagreeable thought. After all the flavor had been boiled out of me they would throw in some schmaltz and chicken-flavored bouillon, then cook me some more! Then, as if to add insult to injury, they would add noodles! *Noodles!*

The thought of being forced to endure the doughy creatures as traveling companions, or of one wrapping itself around the boiled flesh of my prick as I floated in my own broth was really too hideous to bear.

"It must have been very frightening for you," said Tom sympathetically.

"It was. I couldn't breathe, and the chicken was getting scared and started to squirm. I really thought it was all over. Even the audience got nervous."

"How did you save yourself?" asked Tom.

"I kept yanking at his feet, really pulling—and finally I worked him free. At first I thought I had a dead chicken on my hands. He was really limp, his beak hung open and everything. He didn't move a muscle, not even to twitch. But I should have known better. He's a plucky little bastard. Wasn't more than a few seconds until he began flapping and thrashing. I let him loose and he hopped like hell off the stage. Got back a little while ago and he was on his feed sack crowing to be fed. Didn't bother him a bit. As for me, I just stood there, breathing. You have no idea how good air feels until you almost suffocate."

"Perhaps, Señor Nick, there is a reason for your trial."

"Sure there was. I didn't grease my throat like I usually do. I always swallow castor oil. Makes things go down smoothly. Gives me a terrible case of the shits afterwards but it's worth it. Keeps things from getting stuck."

"No Señor, I think there was another more overpowering reason for your brush with death."

"How so?"

"It is a sign from God. He, in His wisdom wants you to see the error of your ways and save yourself before it is too late. He, in His infinite mercy is giving you a chance to repent. How often do you go to church?"

"Never. I am an anarchist."

"Obscure religions are looked upon with disfavor by the Almighty. He has imparted wisdom to Mother Church and to her flock. The others are damned. Give up this false faith you practice, this 'anarchism,' and throw yourself upon the Holy Mother and Blessed Virgin, and be saved. He must love you very much to be taking all this trouble for you."

"But Tom, I *like* being an anarchist."

"The way sinners love sin!" he said sorrowfully. "How they will regret it in eternity!"   .

"Tom, it's your life. You were born into it. I can no more convert than I could turn black. Your little sister Consuela is probably a better follower, even at her age, than I could ever be."

"Ah yes, Consuela is a good girl. Already she knows the teachings and practices them with diligence. Already, even at her tender age, she is pregnant with the Faith, converting new souls in the best way she knows how."

"Isn't she a little young to be pregnant?" asked the Geek.

"Some are brought early to good works, my friend. Already through devotion she is bringing new souls to the altar of Holiness."

"It doesn't seem practical somehow," said the Geek.

"Let Consuela stay with you. Though young, she is wise in the ways of sin, and through sin, salvation. She in her wisdom will save your soul."

"But I don't want my soul saved by an under-aged girl. People have been known to go to prison for that."

"Skeptic! Don't you know God will protect you from prison? He wants to see you saved and will let nothing stand in your way."

"What if God should fuck up and I get caught?" asked the Geek.

"Then take heart. God works in mysterious ways. If He allows you to go to prison it is for a purpose. Perhaps you shall meet salvation there, or bring salvation to someone else."

"But I don't want to find salvation in jail, and I don't want to save any souls in prison. If you want to save men behind bars, you go to jail."

"I leave you with Consuela, my friend. She will save you fast and painlessly."

"But I don't..."

"*Hasta la vista.* You will learn that the faith of my good sister is better than the filth of your anarchists."

With that, Tom the Trapeze Boy slipped through the door of the tent, leaving the Geek to the mercy of the ten-year-old girl. As she wiggled up to him, he backed away.

"Forget it, kid. I'm not messing with any ten-year-olds."

"Señor Nick, do you want to go to hell?"

"Holy shit!" was all he said.

Shortly the door flap separated. The Geek looked up to see one of the chimpanzees standing in it holding a sandwich and a bottle of beer. Pinned to its shirt was a note:

Accept token of sympathy for near miss of afternoon. Salami sandwich and beer should restore faith in ability of throat to swallow. These things happen.

—Harry

P.S. Salami kosher.

The Geek put the food on his collapsible card table and sat down to write a note of thanks to Harry. As his pencil scratched his gratitude across lined tablet paper, the chimp scampered up his leg onto his shoulder. Wrapping his paws firmly around the Geek's head, he stuck his little peter into the hole of the Geek's ear. Its diameter fitted comfortably. The Geek's view as he watched from the corner of his eye was unfortunately obstructed by the side of his face.

The ape made little excited chattering noises and pressed one hairy leg into the flesh of the Geek's cheek. The other leg it braced behind his head, the knee partially hidden in the hair.

His groin beat urgently into the convoluted flap of the Geek's outer ear. The simian's chatterings turned to high pitched squeals as his excitement mounted. His arms clutched the man's head as his hips vibrated electrically. A stream of liquid dribbled out of the Geek's ear. The chimp released its arms, freeing the Geek's head, then somersaulted off the Geek's shoulder onto the floor. He landed on his feet, then hopped excitedly. Clapping his hands and squealing in glee, he turned cartwheels on the floor to the door and out.

The Geek pulled a handkerchief out of his pocket and molded it around his extended middle finger. With it, he scooped into the raped ear to clean it out. He held the soiled cloth in his hand for a few moments, staring at it quizzically before tossing it on the floor. He leaned forward, unfolding the wax paper wrap from the sandwich. He bit deeply into the salami on rye, then devoured it all, chewing with relish.

After he had finished, he leaned back in the chair and pulled a black-market Havana from his pocket and lit it. Inhaling, he held it between two fingers as he reached for and finished the last of his beer.

His head fell back and rolled to one side. His eyes slowly closed. Jaw relaxed and hanging open, he began to snore softly.

Chapter 12

Shortly after the Geek had fallen asleep, I heard running feet outside the tent. A man shouted. The Geek, hearing the commotion, opened his eyes, blinked and craned his neck in the direction of the noise. The evening immediately became quiet. As silence settled over the night he shrugged, leaned back in his seat and closed his eyes again. After a few minutes of silence the canvas of the tent door rippled as a hand reached in through the crack between the knots that tied it shut. Another slipped in above it, holding an open jackknife. This the hand transferred to its mate underneath. Armed, it bent at the wrist enabling the knife to saw the knot below, while the free hand held the rope taut. Thread by thread the weapon cut through.

The top of a head and shoulders followed the hands and arms into the opening. Bending low, the intruder untied the rope below the one it had cut, and then severed the bottom knot. After pushing back the flap, the dark form stepped inside. Alarmed, I began to crow. Whoever it was became perfectly still and crouched low near the opening.

The Geek opened his eyes and squinted at me disgustedly.

"If you don't shut the fuck up, I'm going to wring your skinny pink neck! So *shut up!*"

I crowed again, flapping toward the intruder. I felt a stinging pain on the side of my head as the glass beer bottle bounced off it. All right, I decided, if that's the way he was going to be, to hell with him. I settled back down, totally pissed, to watch the robber or whatever, do his thing.

The shadowy figure stood up after the Geek began to snore again. Lifting his arm high, he motioned for someone else outside the tent to come in. This was beginning to get interesting. Another figure followed, and then another. Five in all stood inside the flap door of the Geek's tent. All were dressed in dark clothing and seemed to be wearing sneakers. They moved soundlessly. One of them untied the kerchief around his neck, while the one behind pulled a length of rope from his pocket. The first, who stood behind the Geek, reached over the sleeping man's head and forced the handkerchief around his mouth, knotting it in back. The Geek jerked forward, and tried to stand, but the others held him down while the one with the rope tied his hands together at the wrists. Part of the rope hung free. The first, taking an open knife out of his pocket, cut it just above the knot, leaving a length several feet long. While his companions held the legs of the squirming captive, the one with the rope walked around the chair to the front and tied the Geek's legs together at the ankles. One of them went out the front door, was gone several minutes, and returned with a long thick pole.

With another length of rope, they tied the Geek to it, his body hanging below. Four of them shouldered it safari-style and marched out of the tent, while the fifth loosely retied the uncut ropes behind them from the inside. He stumbled around, tripping over the clutter and examining objects by touch. Finally he picked up the Geek's battery-operated lamp. His fingers searched its surface. I heard a small click, and the tent filled with light. It illuminated a stocky figure, back turned to me, dressed in a black sweater and black Capri pants. The hair was shoulder length, which struck me as odd. I had heard hippies were gentle people and felt mildly disillusioned at these five, who were anything but gentle. Then the figure turned.

The prowler's face had a cautious expression on it. The black eyes were hard and old and darted from side to side. Swarthy skin with the texture of leather hung from bold cheekbones. The gigantic beaked nose overshadowed the tight-pressed lips under it. The head grew out of a short stubby neck which disappeared under the turtleneck of the black sweater. Jutting out from under its knit were breasts, hard looking and small, but breasts nonetheless.

I squawked in amazement when I realized that the intruder was female.

This proved to be a mistake, since it caught her attention. She lunged at me, both hands extended, and grabbed. I flapped several feet in the air and escaped. She charged bull-like, panting roughly as her hand again swiped out at me. It grazed my tail-feathers and knocked me sideways. I regained my balance and flapped behind the table to the opposite side. She jumped to the right as I hopped to the left, keeping a whole table between us. So far so good. At that moment she thrust the heel of her hand under the top to push it over onto me. I flapped several feet into the air and saved myself from being pinned under it, but in so doing came within reach of her grabbing hands.

She caught me by one leg and held me tight as I struggled, pecking at her. She grabbed me behind the neck with her other hand, just under my head and out of reach from my beak. I struggled, flapping violently and trying to loosen her grip. With a free finger she shut off the light. Walking to the door flap, she stood still, waiting. When she heard only silence she stuffed me under her arm, still holding onto my neck with her left hand, and untied the tent rope. Pushing her head against the canvas she stepped out into the world of the sleeping circus.

Her arm, squeezing my body against hers, had caught my wing in an awkward position cutting off the circulation. In abandoning all hope for escape I gave myself up to the wish that we would get wherever we were going before my wing fell completely asleep. I hung limp, staring glumly at the ground as it passed below my head. We reached the outskirts of the circus. After passing the last tent, I saw an old reconverted dump truck. The cab was like any other, but was attached to a back which had been made over to resemble a covered wagon, with rounded hoops holding up the canvas covering that had been nailed to it. Through a crack I saw a light shining. My captor went to the back and knocked.

"It's me, Stella. I have the chicken. Hurry up and let me in."

The canvas that hung from the top was lifted

and a woman with thick lips and chopped brown hair stuck her head out.

"Come on in. Don't be so nervous."

I was lifted and put into the hands of the other woman. As my captor pulled herself up into the truck, she told what had happened.

"I didn't get caught or seen, I don't think. But the chicken was noisy and I had to push over a table to catch him. I came back as quickly as I could but I didn't want to take any chances."

"Well, the important thing is that you got back in one piece and with the chicken."

After the flap had been securely tied at the bottom, I was let loose. I saw the Geek propped against one corner, still tied up. I flapped over to him and landed on his legs.

"Now isn't that sweet!" said one of them.

I looked around. Four women were crowded into the back along with the Geek and me. All were dressed in black. All had straggly dirty hair, and all were ugly. Coarse-featured, mannish and ugly, UGLY, *UGLY!*

"Well, now that we're all together we might as well push off," said the oldest and ugliest.

She tapped on the back window of the cab. When the shadowy form of the driver turned around, she signaled for the motor to be started. With a lurch, the truck rattled forward.

Chapter 13

For hours the truck bumped along unpaved and winding roads. The jolting made me sick and much to the disgust of my captors, I spat up on the floor.

"First chickenshit, then he throws up. Why couldn't we have used our own hen?"

"Well for one thing, he's pink and goes with the act. It is more exciting that way. Secondly, he's used to the whole scene. Ours isn't and might panic. The Geek would choke, and it might blow the whole thing. We'd have to go through all this again with another geek."

"Go through *what* again?" asked the Geek apprehensively.

"Geek-napping," replied a fat woman of fifty or so whose arm sported a large blue and red tattoo that rippled whenever she flexed her muscles.

"What do you need a geek for?" asked their captive.

"We like your act. It does things for us," she replied.

"What kind of things?" he asked.

"Well, you swallow your chicken and this holds all sorts of symbolic eroticism for us."

"I don't understand," said the Geek frowning.

"First, it is oral. You may or may not have guessed that we are particularly fond of that form of sex. I'm sure, however, that a man of your sophistication figured that out as soon as you laid eyes on us." She lit a cigar and continued her explanation:

"Secondly, the act has oral-genital overtones. The oral, of course is your own rosebud mouth. Simple isn't it? The genital is provided by that lovely pink creature you call a chicken. Its color was a stroke of genius and one of the main reasons why we chose *you* instead of some other geek. It gives the perfect penile touch." She scratched her ass as she talked on:

"Last, and most abstractly is the genital-genital

symbolism. Of course one has to let one's imagination run free in order to appreciate it." After a pause she continued to talk:

"Those, my good Geek, are the main reasons we have kidnapped you. In addition, and it is only of secondary importance, is your value as a touch of variety for our rather jaded sexual palates. Spice, as it were. A steady diet of anything, no matter how pleasant, can be a bit of a bore. For that reason we shall find your (I hope) sturdy and capable cock an ideal seasoning and perfect dessert."

"You mean I swallow for you and then you fuck me?" asked the Geek hopefully.

"Sometimes, but not always," replied the tattooed woman. "Sometimes we just tie you up and whip you or just tie you and let you swallow and watch *us* do it."

"As long as I'm performing, I want some action in return," said the Geek.

"You, my dear, don't have much of a choice. You're more or less a captive audience."

"What if I don't swallow?"

"No swallow, no eat."

"That's dirty," muttered the Geek.

"Thank you."

"Okay, okay, you've got me. I'm stuck whether I like it or not. But answer me something."

"Gladly. What is it you'd like to know?"

"What do *you do* when I swallow him?" he asked, pointing at me.

"You'll see," she answered. "Basically what you'd expect aroused women to do. Use your imagination."

All this excitement was giving me diarrhea, and despite my best efforts I was shitting all over the floor. Even more embarrassing was the condition of the stuff. Runny green and white, it dribbled loosely from my rectum in spurts and gushes. I tried to be as inconspicuous as possible, confining my shits to the floor behind some furniture pads.

Fortunately they never noticed the little pile I had amassed until long after our journey had been completed. By then it was hard and required a knife to scrape it away. I felt a certain satisfaction when I heard it mentioned in conversation. I felt it served them right.

Well, they all rested as the truck lurched along the road. Sleeping in cycles, they took turns driving and the truck went steadily through day as well as night.

One long-haired female who had been asleep curled up in a corner woke up along toward morning. She crawled to the snoring Geek and unzipped his pants. She stuck her hand into the opening, cupping her fingers under the purplish flesh of his scrotum. As she massaged gently, a slumbering smile spread over his sleeping face. He moaned contentedly as his dream took a turn for the better. His pleasure center purred.

Cough center, hunger center, speech center, screw center. Centers touched by day to day commonplaces like being fingered by a bull dyke kidnapper in a speeding reconverted dump truck. His lips rocked to and fro happily under the caress of his captor.

As he lay blissfully sleeping, she pulled a knife out of her pocket and cut away the center seam of his trousers through the zipper and spread the cloth away to expose the bare flesh of hips and groin.

She grabbed the stiffened flesh with a grip of steel and squeezed. He woke with a gasp. She grinned maliciously at his sufferings.

Sweat beaded on his forehead, mingling with tears as her sharpened fingernails dug deeply into the head of his prick, then into the yielding flesh of his balls. He moaned deeply as his body twisted away from her torturing fingers. She dug ever more deeply into his sensitive parts, piercing them with the points of her nails. Blood flowed over her fingertips.

"As you have probably guessed, I am a sadist," she said calmly as her thumbnail sank into the hole from where the piss, and on good days the sperm, flows. The Geek screamed, twisting away from her and sobbing.

"Christ, Sadie!" muttered one of the women through clenched teeth. "If you're going to torture the mother while the rest of us are trying to sleep, at least tie a gag on him."

"All right!" she said and reached for the piece of cloth the women had used earlier. Grabbing it, she tied the gag around his mouth awkwardly.

Sadie unbuckled the belt still clinging to his waist, pulled it from its loops and threw it to the side. Yanking viciously, she pulled the remaining scraps of trousers down from his hips, down his outstretched legs. She left them in a pile around his ankles. His eyes popped as she straddled him, loosely wrapping her own legs around his back. In this position she bent forward, her nose and mouth almost in her own pubic hair. Baring her teeth, she covered the Geek's genitals with her mouth. Biting into him, her jaw steadily crushed his flesh.

The human jaw is capable of applying a bite of one hundred pounds pressure. Judging by the purple color rising in the Geek's face, his bulging eyes and the strangled moan under the gagging handkerchief, I guessed that she was damn near close to the limit. When she straightened, throwing her head back, I saw that her bared teeth were covered with blood. Halfway down the shaft of the

Geek's penis, spurts of it shot out of the open wounds. The rest of the injured organ had taken on a dark purple color and was already beginning to swell. At the top, the head was covered with spit and whitish sperm oozed out of the abused eye.

I shouldn't have been too surprised that he really enjoyed it. I remembered quite vividly the antics between him and his lover the Reptile Man. The Geek enjoyed nothing more than taking whatever was dished out to him. Only the Reptile Man understood this, or if not understanding it, fulfilled it unconsciously when he used the Geek the way all his other partners used him, to fill his own needs. For that reason the Geek adored the Reptile Man and panted for the chance to make love to him. Delightfully violent, painful and bloody was the love the Geek found thrilling despite his protests.

My fondest memories are of the Reptile Man standing over the Geek, silver chain in hand, ripping into the flesh of his slave's back. He would laugh when the Geek begged him to stop, and would slam away harder. The flesh bulged through the crotch of his tights, as the Geek, tied to the pole, sobbed and begged for mercy. His hips would writhe under the lash of the chain. The fluid rolled out of his prick as tears of agony fell from his eyes. The sweat would drip from his armpits. The angry welts on his bruised flesh turned to blisters as the

lash came down again and again on his bare back
and buttocks.

Nostalgic tears spring to my eyes as I remember
the time when the Reptile Man ordered the Geek to
his hands and knees. He climbed onto his back, and
ran the spurs he was wearing into the soft flesh of
his mount's ass. As the sharp points punctured his
skin the Geek screamed, collapsed his arms, and
hit his chin on the floor. The Reptile Man spurred
harder, ordered him up, then reached back and
slapped the bloody rump with his open palm. The
Geek straightened and crawled around the tent on
his hands and knees while the rider continually
slapped his ass. When the time came to tether his
horse, the Reptile Man wrapped a length of twine
around the Geek's now hardened prick. He tied it
tightly enough to make the flesh on either side
bulge, knotted it and fastened the other end to a
tent pole. The prick, with its hot blood and boiling
sperm trapped under the twine, turned purple. The
Geek, too terrified to disobey, remained on his
hands and knees playing horse, while the Reptile
Man poured and drank a shot of whiskey.

After he had finished, he sauntered over to the
Geek and stuck his huge prick into the rectum.
Straddling from behind, his pelvis beat against
flesh and knocked off pieces of dried blood as he
pounded. The flesh of the Geek's own prick grew

darker and more purple as it strained against the twine binding.

I happened to hear voices from the corner and turned my attention to the matter immediately. Sadie was stroking the Geek's injury and crooning.

"Poor baby. You got hurt. We'll have to do something about that, won't we?"

She smiled sweetly while she lifted the top off the cooler. Reaching in she scooped out a handful of ice. Cupping her hand she let the ground ice spill over into both hands then clapped them around the bruised and fevered flesh. His eyes widened as she pulled her hands down the shaft to the bottom, to press it hard into his balls.

Quick-frozen scrotum!

Place frozen meat into two-thirds cup boiling water. Cover and bring again to boil. Simmer for about ten minutes over low heat, until product can be pierced easily with fork. Do not refreeze.

The dyke sadist reached again, this time into a large picnic basket and pulled from it a fork. She slipped her fingers under the wrinkled flesh of his pre-frozen balls. With her free hand she pronged them with the eating utensil, not hard enough to draw more blood, but close.

The Geek shrank away and stared in bug-eyed horror at her and at the fork she wielded. She smiled coyly and looked sideways into his eyes as she dug into the flesh again and again, pronging playfully. Laughingly she threw the knife on the floor. After nipping the head of his penis one more time she retreated again to a corner and fell asleep.

The Geek sat still, pants around his ankles. The melting ice left the flesh of his penis shiny and glistening. By now the lady with the tattoo had awakened to watch with interest the Geek's discomforts. In fact, her little pig eyes literally gleamed as they focused on his dripping, sagging prick. A resolute expression crossed her face and she crawled to the helpless man.

She sat on his legs facing him. Dropping her jaw, she strained it to open wide. She exhaled forcefully then put her mouth over his to cover it completely. She opened his lips with her tongue, running it along his upper bridge to explore his molars and tickle his gums.

"My, what bad breath you have," said the Geek, gagging, when she lifted her mouth from his.

"All the better to offend you with!" replied the dyke, cheerfully blowing on his nose.

"Have you tried Colgate 100, the mouthwash for lovers?" he persisted politely.

"Don't be a loser!" she replied with contempt in her voice. "If you persist in picking on my breath I shall continue to kiss you. I will blow in your face for the remainder of the trip."

"You have *lovely* breath!" said the Geek.

"Of course!" she said as she pulled herself away from him to sit further down toward his feet.

"You're cutting off my circulation," said the Geek as she settled her one-hundred-fifty-odd pounds on his shinbones.

"You won't even notice it once I get started," she said.

She opened her mouth wide again and bent over his drooping prick.

"My what a big mouth you have!" said the Geek.

"All the better to eat you with!" replied the dyke as she sank her teeth into the shaft of his penis, below the head, and gnawed the tip.

"Why don't you go further down?" asked the Geek. "It feels better for me when you swallow as much as you can."

"The head tastes the best. That, dear man is a direct quote from the immortal Zap Comics. Great truths are uttered in jest. Some of the profoundest philosophy can be found in comic strips, like that immortal morsel of truth I just uttered."

"You may be right," said the Geek. "Fritz the Cat speaks the glorious truth of hedonism."

"Not to mention the unreality and transience of material objects. The toilet he kills during the Great Bathtub Bust is destroyed but transforms into a flowing and living entity that symbolizes life as it ebbs and flows all over the bathroom floor. Then it sinks into the cracks of the bathroom tile to disappear forever. From there it drips off the ceiling below to water the heads of all who live there, *and* the cockroaches, allowing them to live and grow. The roaches in turn spawn children, then die to return to the soil, while their offspring live on.

"Some of the water from the murdered toilet evaporates then turns to rain, watering the flowers of the field and crops. The cycle of life continues forever, all because Fritz the Cat killed the toilet."

"It's allegorical," said the Geek as he wiped a tear from his eye. "I see now that Snuffy Smith is another example. Without putting it into words, the creator has succeeded in showing the beauty of the honest peasant in his fight against the cruel establishment."

"Ah yes. Snuffy and his friends living their own lives so heroically under the dark shadow of the Government. They created their own folk art while living in mortal fear that the Revenoors and their wicked government-issue axes will destroy it. Ah yes, they too know the cruel lash of the Washington monarchy."

"Another," said the Geek, "is Snoopy. A cult hero, he preaches by example the esoteric philosophy of pure solipsism."

"Yes, the truly great comic strip characters show

by example in their very life styles, the philosophies and political ideals that lesser men have to write manifestos to express."

"I still wish you'd swallow the whole thing when you blow me," muttered the Geek.

When his penis was fully erect she lifted herself off his legs. Spreading the lips of her cunt wide with both hands, she lowered herself onto him, letting his prick sink deep in her flesh.

"My what a big cunt you have!" said the Geek.

"All the better to fuck you with!" replied the tattooed woman defensively.

"Not really," replied the Geek. "I don't feel a thing. You're too large."

"No, my dear Geek," she replied, her temper rising. "The problem is you're too small."

"I never had any complaints before," muttered the Geek in a snit, his vanity wounded.

"You never laid any honest women before."

"A stretched woman is not necessarily an honest woman."

"Your problem is that you've laid too many circus freaks. And now you don't know anything else."

She ground her meat in a circular motion over the Geek's erection. She pulled herself off and said sarcastically:

"Thy rod and thy staff comfort me." She stood up. The dripping hairs of her cunt brushed his mouth.

"Thou preparest a table before me in the presence of mine enemies," said the Geek as he inserted his tongue into the slick wetness, lapping the juices that dripped out of her.

She wrapped her hands around his head, pressing closer to enable him to dig more deeply into her with his tongue. As the pink muscle darted in and out she wiggled her hips into his face.

Head thrown back, she chanted "Louie Louie," hips grinding in rhythm to the words as they worked a little cooch-dance into the pink tongue of the Geek.

Suddenly her thighs locked and the muscles of her cunt gripped the Geek, imprisoning his tongue inside her. He tried to protest but could make only muffled indignant noises instead. Just as suddenly as she imprisoned him, she spread her legs and relaxed the muscles to free the Geek. As he gasped to regain his breath, she stood, cunt directly over his head and drenched him with a stream of hot urine. She squatted and pressed the lips of her opening against his soaked hair, savoring the friction against her soft insides.

"Does that turn you on?" asked the Geek sarcastically.

"Yes."

"What about me?"

"What *about* you?"

"It doesn't turn *me* on."

"So?"

"So don't I have any rights?"

"No."

When she had aroused herself on his head, she stood and walked over to a youngish woman.

"Clea," she said, "lie back."

Clea obeyed. The tattooed woman crouched over her and let the bush of her lower region rest on the girl's mouth. She adjusted her weight, resting on her knees instead of the balls of her feet, and rocked back and forth into the girl's waiting mouth. Clea sucked the older woman's juices, slurping noisily as her hands clutched at the rump shaking passionately above her, the fatty humps of the cheeks confined within her iron grip. Their bodies rolled in unison like a well-oiled machine and their breath became, when they bothered to breathe, hoarse and labored. Perspiration wet their flesh as the mouths of each sucked and licked the vagina of the other. Fingernails dug into flesh as each reached orgasm.

Chapter 14

The truck screeched to a halt, its wheels grinding against the gravel topping of the deserted country road. After the engine stopped sputtering, I could hear breakers crashing on land. A mixture of salt and oil odors mingled in the air. I knew we must be on the beach. A coarse female voice yelled orders to someone far away.

"Over here!" she rasped. "Bring it close and hold it!"

A motor putted louder and louder then died out, coughing.

"They're in the truck," she shouted, her footsteps padding toward the truck.

The tattooed woman, whom they called Big Maria, grabbed me by the neck then scooped me up under her arm. The canvas back of the wagon was untied by the woman outside. She threw the flap onto the top of the wagon. Big Maria, with me securely under her arm, jumped out. Out of the corner of my eye I could see the Geek being dragged from the truck, his arms held by two muscular women. They had untied his feet. Despite his stubborn refusal to walk, they managed to drag him toward the boat anchored in the tiny lagoon.

Gripping him tightly they waded out and pushed him up into it. There he was promptly grabbed by the three women inside. Two of them held him down while the third yanked the rope to start the motor. Maria struggled through the water still carrying me. As it rose up past her waist my beak came closer to touching the sea. I was afraid that I would drown before we got there. Fortunately, by holding my head high I managed to survive. Big Maria lifted me to the waiting hands of the operator while she herself climbed over the side, tipping the boat as she pulled her body up and over. She lay panting on the floor for several minutes. When she finally revived she took me once more from the driver. When she had me securely in her hands the boatman throttled the engine and the boat roared forward. We rocked in the choppy water until I thought my gullet would turn inside out. The Geek doubled over and groaned softly, looking very pale. I wasn't feeling any too good myself. I was about to spit up the crummy barnyard seed they had fed me in the truck. Nausea tightened my insides as the molten mass of half-digested feed rolled up my throat, out my beak and onto the tattooed woman.

"Shit!" she said, wiping it from her hairy arm.

"Oh God!" said the driver. "A seasick chicken!"

"He's not the only one," said Maria pointing at the Geek, who was leaning over the side of the boat and heaving the contents of his insides into the murky sea water.

"You can probably let go of the bird," said one of the others. "Chickens can't swim. They're only good for hopping around a barnyard and laying eggs."

Well, at that I promptly forgot my seasickness and my fear. If they had any sense they'd know I couldn't lay eggs even if I *were* a common barnyard fowl. Only abysmal ignorance could have confused me with a *hen. I* promptly set to crowing. I would show them exactly how wrong they were. Maria, less dense than the others, got the idea.

"I think he's trying to tell us that he doesn't lay eggs," she said laughing. "He fucks hens."

Don't I wish! I thought glumly. It was hard

trying to live up to a reputation not of your own making. I wondered what they'd think if they knew I had never even been *near* a hen. Circus life had its drawbacks, despite the glamour.

"How are you feeling?" Big Maria asked the Geek.

A long low groan escaped from his lips. His shoulders, hunched over the side of the boat, began to heave violently. He made gagging, retching sounds. The water below him splashed as the contents of his stomach hit and sank. He left behind him a foamy trail of food as the boat sped forward.

"Ah ah ah ah ah!" moaned the Geek. "Where the hell are we going?"

He threw up again into the water.

"To the island," replied one of the dykes.

"How much longer?" groaned the Geek.

"Couple of hours," replied his captor cheerfully, as she tore into a sausage sandwich with her teeth.

"Oh God!" muttered the Geek, gagging. "I can't stand it!"

"It'll be over before you know it," she said consolingly.

"I doubt it," he groaned, leaning over the side of the boat. "I already know it."

"You'll like it when we get there," she said. "You'll feel very much at home on our nice escape-proof island."

"You're leasing maybe Alcatraz?" asked the Geek sarcastically, his head dangling near the water.

"Not quite, but it'll do. It's a nice long swim to shore and we won't be keeping any boats with us."

"Don't mention boats. I can't stand the sight or sound of them right now."

"You'll probably feel differently once you forget how lousy you feel right now."

The Geek pulled himself back into the boat and lay on the floor, gagging.

The dirty salt water sloshing around in the bottom soaked his clothes as he wallowed in his sickness. He closed his eyes and lay very still.

Eventually the females stopped talking and settled into a sleepy lull as the boat sped forward. Maria released her hold on me and began to stare vacantly into the sea. I perched on a wooden slat and went to sleep.

I was awakened by a change in speed. We were slowing down as the water became choppier. I opened one eye and saw that we were heading toward a little harbor surrounded on three sides by land. We finally stopped near shore. Two of the women pulled the Geek up from the bottom and out of the boat, dragging him through the shallow water to dry land. Maria tucked me under her arm and joined them. The closer we came, the faster the women could walk. Soon the breakers covered only the tops of their feet, and they could progress easily.

Waiting for us on shore was a group of about ten to twelve women, all hefty, all stark naked. They crowded around us as we reached the dry sand of the beach. A large, slippery looking woman wearing only gigantic gold hoop earrings stood in front of the Geek. She threw her arms around him, goosing him from behind. He moaned and rolled his eyes to the sky in unbearable pain.

"What's with him?" she asked Maria.

"Been puking all the way over. Seasick."

"Pretty unhealthy specimen!" said the woman, studying the grayish goose-pimpled flesh of his bare loins. "Think he'll live?"

"Yeah. It's just the sea and unhealthy habits. A few hours in the sun, exercise and some health food and he'll be good as new."

"Ah ah ah ah ah!" moaned the Geek. "What is this place anyway?"

"It's the Sunshine Sappho Health Retreat," she replied proudly, "one of America's only two underground nudist camps, and sister camp to the Gaylord Sunshine and Health Spa, located on another island about ten miles away. Sometimes we get together and hold costume dances. Both groups come in drag and socialize."

"Charming," said the Geek. "That's your recreation when you get tired of all that sunshine and fresh air, I suppose."

"Part of it," she replied, ignoring his sarcasm. "You're part of it too."

"So I've been told," said the Geek glumly.

"You, the dances and the good fellowship of each other, in the healthful salt-air setting of this lovely island, remote enough to guarantee privacy."

"A regular country club," muttered the Geek.

"Don't be sarcastic!" replied the woman. "Of course it's exclusive. We want to make sure we get only the right kind of person. To get in, you have to be recommended by two campers in good standing. Then your background is investigated and your status in our community verified." She stared at him and continued. "If all that is satisfactory, then you are given a thorough physical examination. If your body is found to be to the liking of those doing the examining, then you are voted on. If you should be blackballed, you can forget about ever joining. Nobody loves a loser."

"How impressive."

"It keeps us out of jail." She turned to Maria. "He doesn't look as if he'll be much good for awhile. Take him to the hut and get him settled. I want him fresh for tonight."

"Who are you anyway?" asked the Geek.

"I'm Roxie the Recreation Director."

"Come on," said Maria, slapping the Geek's flabby ass with the palm of her free hand.

She held it there, squeezing one cheek. By the pressure of her hand on his flesh, she guided him to the hut. From my view under her arm, I could see we were approaching the wooded area, covered with palm, coconut, bamboo, and avocado of all sizes, as well as some underbrush I didn't recognize. We walked down a path that had been cut through the wilderness until we came to a grass-roofed hut made of bamboo poles tied together with vines.

"It's humble, but it's home," said Big Maria with a sweeping gesture of her hand. "I hope you'll find it comfy."

"I'm sure I will," muttered the Geek sullenly, "but I miss my circus."

"A natural homesickness, but one you'll get over in a week or less. We'll make you feel very welcome."

They crouched to get in through the door. Once inside they straightened up. Their heads nearly touched the roof. It was kind of pleasant in a way, all tan and rustic. On the floor was thrown a thick grass mat and woolen blanket. A candle in a tin holder was set on an orange crate in the middle of the room.

"Don't get any wild ideas about burning up the island," warned Maria. "We installed a water pump and if anything happens on this side, we'll know who did it. If you try to hide, we'll find you. It's a small island. And when we find you, we'll be really pissed. Especially if you did a lot of damage. Understand?"

"I understand. I hadn't any definite plans for that sort of thing anyway, at least not until I get a few hours sleep."

"Good. Now we'll be back for you later. Have a good rest and remember what I told you."

She left the Geek and me alone in the hut. He groaned then curled up on the mat, pulling the blanket over his head. Soon he began to snore.

Despite my growling stomach, I was tired from the excitement. I fluffed my feathers and drew in my head. I too fell asleep.

Chapter 15

Footsteps outside the hut crashed through the underbrush that hung over the path. I opened my eyes and saw that it was twilight. Bodies pushed in through the doorway.

"Wake up!" shouted a female voice.

The Geek groaned and pulled himself further under the shelter of his woolen blanket.

"Rise and shine!" shouted another woman as she yanked the blanket away from him. Two of them grabbed his arms and jerked him to his feet.

"Take off his shirt!" ordered another. A small-breasted woman with a strawberry birthmark on her shaven cunt ripped the shirt off his back, sending buttons flying in all directions.

"Not too hairy!" she remarked, staring at his chest. "I really wish he had more hair."

"We can't satisfy all fetishes at once," answered Maria, while her hand explored the crack of his ass.

"You never do," sighed the disappointed fetishist. "The last geek was bald."

"Be thankful for small favors. This one isn't!" said a companion consolingly.

"But he has no body hair. That's what makes the man, body hair."

"Oh I wouldn't say that," remarked another in the crowd.

"Different points of view," countered Maria, ever objective.

"Just once I'd like to get my teeth into someone with a good chest of hair," sulked the fetishist.

"We'll kidnap a gorilla!" said another, giggling.

"Cutie-pie!" muttered the hair-loving woman.

A large negress, wearing only the yellow and white flowers that were painted on her nipples, knelt in front of the slumping Geek. She took his prick and held it between her lips. As she sucked, more of its length disappeared into her mouth. Her jaws circled in a chewing motion. The flesh under her cheekbones puckered as the muscles pulled at the limp flesh of his prick.

The Geek smiled. He seemed pleased with the attention he was receiving. He put his hands on top of her head and began to massage the fur-covered scalp. She moaned with pleasure as he ran his fingers down her ears to the back of her neck. His hips rolled, slowly pressing into her head. Her tongue licked and rolled around his ever-hardening prick. His hands clutched the back of her head. He pressed her face harder into his own groin. Running her hands up his legs to his rump she began to squeeze and press the flabby flesh with her strong dark fingers. The Geek moaned and bent down, burying his face in her afro. He nuzzled in the ebony fuzz and savored the feel of its texture against the skin of his cheeks. She pressed four of her long fingers deep into the rosebud opening of his anus to explore his large intestine. He moaned, his whole body writhing against her head. He grabbed mouthfuls of her hair and sucked it between the tongue and roof of his mouth. He came, pouring his thick sticky liquid into her waiting mouth. As she swallowed, he cried out:

"You're beautiful! Do you know that? You're really beautiful!"

"Yeah, I know."

"I mean it. In all sincerity, you are great! What's your name?"

"Angelfood."

"It figures. Myths always have a basis in reality."

Angelfood laughed softly, smiling at him seductively.

"You know, whiteman, you aren't bad." She gave his drooping penis one final lick and stood up. "You even taste good."

As she walked away he stared with pleasure at her rounded, pinchable hips.

"No wonder they made you illegal!"

"Do your thing!" she called out cryptically as she crouched through the doorway to disappear into the growing darkness. He watched until she was no longer visible, then turned to Maria.

"I'm hungry. And if you don't feed *that*," he said pointing at me, "he'll drive us all crazy."

"You get dinner in the clearing. That's what we came for."

I was overjoyed. My insides were turning inside out from the lack of food. I had my heart set on some lovely hemp, but I knew better than to expect miracles. I would probably get some more barnyard shit. Still, food was food, and I was hungry.

We were led down a path to a clearing. Six picnic tables were set up. Most of the nudists were already seated, stuffing themselves. The Geek and the others joined them, completely forgetting about me! I watched in outraged amazement as they crammed the food into their mouths. I decided to remind them. I crowed loudly. Then I crowed again in my most earsplitting tones. One of the women turned to the Geek.

"Isn't there some way to shut it up?"

"Feed him. He won't stop until he gets fed. He's always like that when he's hungry."

A tall plain one with the most amazingly saggy boobs crawled from under her bench. She stood up and walked over to a large sack. Opening it she reached in and pulled out a handful of grain. I devoured it all when she threw it at me. Still hungry, I began to crow for more.

"How much does he get?" she asked the Geek.

"About three fistfuls."

She threw two more onto the ground in front of me and sat back down to finish her dinner. The grain was bad, lousy and uneatable, but I was starving. Not having eaten for the whole day, I overcame my distaste and ate all of it. I perched on a pile of wood and let dinner digest.

After they had finished cleaning up the dishes, they moved the tables out of the clearing and piled them up in one corner under a shelter. It was then that I noticed the pole that had been planted in the ground, sticking erect in the center of the clearing.

Two muscular women grabbed the Geek's arms and dragged him over to it. They pressed him against it and tied him with rope. Only his arms were left free.

"What is this supposed to prove?" he asked.

"Merely showmanship," replied one of the husky women. "It heightens the effect if you are tied up."

"Oh."

The electric light tied to the top of the pole was trained on him as if it were a spotlight. The other bulbs scattered throughout the clearing were of a lower wattage and lent an eerie effect to the surroundings. One woman had sneaked up and grabbed me from behind. She walked over to the Geek and handed me to him.

"Swallow!" she ordered.

I looked at the woman. They were by now huddled expectantly around me in a semicircle. The Geek lifted me high and held me by my legs. He turned me around so that I was in my customary position facing him, and lowered me down head first into his open mouth. His teeth glowed in the light of the electric bulb. Inside his mouth was darkness, pure black except for the highlights where the rays of the bulb hit the moisture on his tongue. My head touched his slippery moist flesh. My body pushed into the tightness past the lips. Once again my flesh, caressed by the liquid suction inside, pulled me inward, deeper into the wet darkness of his body. Pulling downward, the muscles grabbed me, imprisoning me, dragging me toward oblivion. Breathless I waited, feeling surrounded. My excitement grew. With a rush he pulled me out, pulled against my feathers, pulled against the slick muscles of his throat. I dangled, covered with wet as the women applauded, cheered.

They were a good audience. They appreciated my courage and skill. I acknowledged their adoration by crowing. Now as usual, I was excited, breathing hard and the proud possessor of a full erection. The evening was yet young and I had hopes for a satisfying ending. I looked around from on high. It was too dark to see out into the crowd. Finally the Geek lowered me and let go. I flapped away feeling sorry for him being tied up the way he was, but not sorry enough to waste any time about it.

Once on the ground, after my eyes had adjusted to the darkness, I saw that the ladies had been busy. One was lying on her back and groaning, the fingers of one hand pressed deep into her cunt, pumping. Her moisture caught the beam from the dim electric light hanging on a tree above her. She massaged the hungry gap inside her body.

Big Maria and Angelfood were together on the ground. Maria, busy sucking the tips of Angelfood's gigantic boobs, drew the dusky nipples into enormous puckered points. The amazon spade lady, her legs wrapped around the hefty torso of Maria, held on tightly with her legs while her spine arched backwards as she writhed. The tall skinny woman who had fed me dinner climbed on top of Angelfood with an ivory dildo strapped to her hips, and pierced into the crack between the luscious cheeks of the negress's buttocks. Pressing with the machine, in and out, her hands reached around Angelfood's sturdy thighs, past the downy fur below her stomach and into the wet opening of her dripping vagina. Cramming as many fingers as she could fit into the jelly-like pastry slit of the spade woman, she kneaded, molding the heated flesh to her eager fingertips. Every muscle of her hand pressed and prodded Angelfood's pubic opening and her fingertips became coated with the scented juices oozing grandly out of the woman's excited flesh. Angelfood moaned ecstatically as the woman pressed down on her, satisfying her lusts.

Hips jerking, vibrating electrically, her body pushed forward on Maria's fingers, crushing them with her weight. As the flesh-covered bones of the skinny one pressed onto her from above, Angelfood screamed in climax, and shuddered to fall limp over Maria underneath.

"Oh baby, you can really do it!" she moaned to both at once before she passed out cold.

By now my own prick was really red hot and just throbbing to be played with, bitten, hand-jobbed, swallowed and even fucked! The pressure was not only building up inside my prick, but inside my head as well. If I didn't get relief and soon, I would be up a wall. It felt as if it weighed a ton. I hopped, weighted down by its volume, and happened upon a masochist laying on the ground, moaning as another woman lay on top, gnawing on her breasts. The blood flowing from her wounded nipples spurted out of the tooth-marked holes. The dark liquid ran down the tender mounds and marked her pale flesh with highway map lines. It dripped onto the ground to soak into the sandy soil. The woman on top dug her fingernails into the soft flesh of her victim's shoulders and pressed until the skin broke. Blood welled up over her fingertips. She grabbed between her teeth a small piece of flesh at the base of the masochist's neck and bit down on it. She missed the jugular vein by a fraction of an inch.

"Oh God, Sadie!" moaned the masochist. "Do it again! Suck it!"

She threw her hands around the neck above her and screamed.

"Devour me!"

She lifted her neck to the woman's bared teeth.

"Drink my blood! It's good for you. Oh please..."

She fell back, moaning softly. The excitement must have been too much for her.

Sadie, being obliging, bent over and placed her

lips on the opening of the girl's neck. She drank deeply, pausing every once in awhile to smack her lips noisily.

"Good!" she said and put her mouth over the flowing wound again. The hair between Sadie's legs was glistening and had wet the flesh of her inner thighs. Once more I heard her lips smack with relish.

She lifted her face off the neck beneath and ran her teeth down the woman's torso to the bushy hair of her cunt. She too was dripping. Sadie pressed her face into the damp of her dark curly pubic mop. She sucked with relish, then drew up and inserted her fingers into the passive body beneath her, churning in and out. When they were thoroughly wet she put them in her mouth, and licked them one by one on all sides. When she had finished, she cleaned her fingernails with her bottom teeth, examining each in the dim electric light as she finished.

"Up the wall, motherfucker!" screamed a woman as she leaped out of the darkness to land on Sadie. She threw her arms roughly around the waist of the sadist, cupping her hands over the breasts of the woman she had grabbed, pressing and squeezing roughly.

"Fuck you, Cleo!" shouted her prey angrily. "Leave me alone!"

Her attacker paid her no heed.

"Goddamn it!" yelled the outraged Sadie. "I *told* you to leave me alone!"

She jammed her elbow into her attacker's gut, twisting her body for maximum effect.

Cleo gasped as the air was driven from her lungs. She doubled over and landed on her back.

Sadie jumped on her and beat her face with clenched fist. Her hand crashed with a thud on the side of her cheek. Cleo, trapped underneath, grabbed a handful of her assailant's hair and yanked it out, then jammed her hand under the woman's chin to push her head backwards with the sickening pock of flesh against flesh.

As Sadie was caught off balance, Cleo slammed the heels of both hands into the chest of the helpless sadist, which caused her to fall back and land on the still reclining masochist who screamed loudly and in pleasure at the pain of being landed on.

The thin woman leaped to her feet and kicked the sadist in the cunt twice, the second time forcing her off the body of the masochist.

The attacker, in indiscriminate rage, kicked the inert figure of the painloving passive, who lay moaning joyfully as the foot slammed against her breasts and thighs. The attacker, while beating the body beneath her, landed her toes in the slit of the masochist's vagina to bury them deep in the passage of her womb. The muscles of her passage, responding to her frenzied pleasure, tightened sharply in reflex to grab hold of the toes, trapping them in the wet and dripping passageway of her body.

She locked her thighs around her attacker's ankle, squeezing them against the knobby bone. Pressing down she covered the arch of her attacker's foot with her hot flesh, while clasping the toes tight within her throbbing, boiling flesh.

Tossing her head from side to side and moaning wildly, she lifted her body and threw her arms around the leg above. She grabbed the thigh, tightly clutching then pulling the woman down on top of her while her hips and cunt pushed against her foot. The woman fell on her with a crash, winded her, and freed her own foot from the masochist's cunt. She lay still, piled on top and breathing hoarsely while the masochist gasped for breath. The hands of the woman below began to explore, pressing slowly into the thighs of her attacker, running them over the cheeks of her ass and up her back. She slowly slid fingers up her backbone to her neck. With one finger she stroked in a circle behind Cleo's ear.

Cleo's legs stirred with life to wrap slowly around the torso of the woman beneath, while she pressed knees into her sides.

The masochist slid her open palms down the

woman's back to her rump, pressing the fingertips of both hands into the crack between the cheeks of her buttocks. She prodded deeply with a steady rhythm, running her fingernails and fingertips around the soft inner wall. The girl beneath flexed the muscles of her rump, squeezing together tightly, then loosening to tighten again, drawing her hips up, under, and around the probing hand.

With her own hands she massaged the woman's shoulders, pressing them over the collarbones and down around the breasts. She rolled the breasts between her fingers, squeezing the tips with the ball of her thumb and her forefinger.

Even in the dim electrical light I could see the masochist's nipples darken and harden to attention, becoming large points at the very edge. Good enough to bite off. At least that's what her attacker must have thought because she bit one neatly between her teeth. Her victim groaned and smiled as the muscles of her hips and loins contracted. She stiffened off the ground then relaxed. Her body slammed up and down against the ground and out of control for several minutes before she relaxed with a sigh, her body still as if dead. Her eyes were closed and she smiled.

The sadist lay to one side, looking crushed and left out. I was tempted to hop over and see if she were still alive and maybe cheer her up if I could. I thought better of it, however, since I didn't know if her sex life ran to chickens as well as women.

Viewing the scene did nothing for my problem, making it worse if anything. My poor prick weighed me down so that I could hardly keep my balance. Only with the greatest effort did I manage to keep from falling forward.

Several feet on, in the shadows, lay the hair fetishist alone, clutching to her a wiglet of dark and somewhat ratty curls. She slid it with feather-light strokes over her boobs. With it she tickled the very tips of her nipples teasing them with the fluffiest curls. She slipped the hair down her neck, tickling it on the side below her earlobes, slowly and gently. Her eyes were closed and a soft, gentle expression covered her face. Cooing softly, she ran the wiglet down her cleavage to her stomach. Slowly and gently she lowered it to her cunt. Legs spread wide, she softly dusted the flesh of her clit, teasing it and gently tormenting it with the curls.

As she lay moaning, tears of disappointment sprang to her eyes.

"If only it were *real!*"

She rolled her head from side to side, sobbing.

"Everyone here is so damned *bald*. Only Angelfood has good hair and she won't let me. Why couldn't they get a geek with hair?"

Tears streamed down her cheeks.

"Pay good money for a trip to camp and what do you get? You don't even get what you pay for." Her body wracked with sobs. "Been better off staying in Venice. At least I could have paid some hippies."

She groaned again as she delicately dusted the lips of her cunt with hair. I felt truly sorry for her. I hopped to her side to see if there were some way I could make her life easier. I thought perhaps feathers would help. I spread my left wing while facing her, and ran it across her stomach as I stood in the shadow of her outstretched armpit. I was careful to be gentle, knowing, or at least surmising, that it is important to a hair fetishist. I stroked her with a slow, light touch. Finally my effort paid off.

"Feels good," she cooed. "What a dear sweet chicken you are."

She picked me up and stroked my comb. It felt good.

"It's not like hair but it's better than my wiglet. I wonder if I could get you to do my neck."

Always glad to help out, I stood on the ground beside her neck and lifted my wing over her neck, bringing it down slowly to let the soft feather tips tickle the sensitive flesh beneath her ear.

"Mmmmmmm!"

Suddenly a flash of inspiration slapped me in the tail feathers. I hopped onto her neck and reached over her chin. While brushing her cheeks with my feathers I managed with a lot of straining and reaching to slip my hardened throbbing cock between her closed lips. If I played my cards right, she would never notice. I hoped. Slowly, trying not to be obvious, I stirred my rigid prick against the firm flesh of her lips. While churning it to relief, I distracted her with the tips of my wing feathers until the flesh of my prick, pushing back and forth, drew the sperm up and out of me and into her.

I played it cool and bridled my relief and passion. I slowly eased it out, careful to make no sudden movements. If she noticed the liquid that had spurted into her mouth, she must have thought it was her own spit or sweat because she didn't move or get angry. Her eyes closed and she smiled.

I was happy. Weak with relief I hopped down her stomach to her leg, and off. As I flapped away, I heard her call after me.

"Here chicken, come back!"

She lazily waved her arm as I turned to look over my shoulder at her. When I didn't come to her she merely sighed and went to sleep.

By now Big Maria had released herself from Angelfood's limp body. She leaped to her feet, shouting:

"The Geek! Let's fuck the Geek!"

Raising her clenched fist high above her head, she flexed her arm at the elbow. She leaped, clicked her heels twice off the ground, and landed on her feet. She charged the Geek shouting at the top of her lungs.

"Gangbusters! Remember Fort Dix! Let's fuck the Geek!"

I was rather surprised at her behavior until I noticed an empty Four Roses bottle on the ground near the prone carcass of Angelfood.

She threw herself upon the Geek. She wrapped her arms and legs around him, pole and all, and hung, supported only by her own muscles. She droolingly kissed him on the mouth, smacking with her own wet thick lips his teeth and the bristles of his mustache. She licked his cheeks with her tongue, ran it up the bridge of his nose to the inner corners of his eyes, to taste and savor the crud that collected there.

"Tear ducts are a delicacy with some aboriginal tribes, you know," she said offhandedly.

"Splendid!" said the Geek. "You're squashing my balls. Could you scoot up or shift your weight and discuss anthropology later?"

"Oh sure," said Maria as she disentangled her legs from his hips.

She stood on the ground still facing him, with her arms wrapped around his neck, and urged her groin onto his. The gentle insistent pressure of her body against his revived his tired genitals and they slowly twitched to life.

With hesitant starts the shaft slowly hardened. Its pressure against her grew more insistent, then urgent as it sought out the object of its need. It pressed blindly for an opening, prodding her stomach and searching for the secret passage to satisfaction that couldn't be found anywhere near her belly button.

Maria understood. Clasping her hands more tightly around the Geek's neck and holding onto the pole for support, she lifted her legs off the ground. Straining the muscles of her stomach and back, she painfully raised her limbs until the soles of her feet pressed into the rough wooden pole behind for support. She hoisted herself high enough so that her vagina was on a level with his hungry, throbbing penis.

"Hold..." she gasped. "Hold onto me, dammit."

The Geek pressed her to him tightly, holding her around the waist as she shoved her gaping cunt down onto the turgid flesh of his prick. The sudden filling of void with volume caused a curious smacking sound, and the plunging of his organ within her made a bubbling noise until her insides sealed around him. Hanging from his neck, held tightly by his strong arms, she forced herself into perfect motionlessness, letting only the small but powerful muscles of her opening massage him.

Her ass twitched in barely noticeable contractions, thrusting toward him as she wrapped her legs around his waist even more tightly. Giving herself up to slow, steady gyrations, she rolled, then became still again, clutching him tightly.

Slowly she released her arms, still keeping her legs tightly bundled around his hips, and arched her back away from his body to lower herself slowly until the crown of her head almost touched the ground below. Her arms fell limp and trailed in the dirt. She hung this way while around her the inhabitants of the island revived from their rest. Growing tired of each other, they turned to the Geek. Finally one of them, after sitting cross-legged on the ground and twiddling her thumbs, stood up and walked over to Maria. She stood over her, staring in helpless bewilderment. Then her eyes brightened and she stooped over and stood on her head to face the dangling woman eye to eye.

"Maria, it's our turn. You've had him long enough," she said.

"I just got started!"

"You look pretty finished to me," said the woman whose face was growing progressively redder. "You can find something else to do! Come on."

"Oh all right," muttered Maria. "Why don't they ration food instead of Geeks?"

Maria braced her arms on the ground below her head and pushed herself off the Geek's body. With her feet against the pole behind him, she landed with a thud on her stomach. When she had freed herself from him, the others careened wildly toward him. Uttering Indian war whoops, they threw themselves upon his tied and trussed body. One of them untied the ropes that bound him with her teeth, jerking them away from his limbs with a toss of her head. The others, still shrieking, pulled him bodily away from the pole and threw him onto the ground. One of them leaped open-mouthed onto his cock, biting and gnawing at it hungrily. He screamed as she ground it with her molars and he twisted away from her.

Sadie the sadist, still on her vampire kick, bit his neck and began slurping noisily at his blood. Cleo straddled one of his legs and writhed, jamming her skinny cunt hard upon it. The masochist sat on his head, and thrust her clit into his mouth between his unwilling teeth.

"Bite me! Bite me!" she cried out, grinding herself onto his tongue. His jaws clamped together on her and she screamed. He released her clit, then clamped down again before she could escape. She screamed again. Her body pressed onto him with hunger as she snapped down again and again. Once she almost escaped and he bit down on her harder than ever. She fainted and fell off of his head. Another woman with masochist leanings kicked her out of the way and climbed onto his mouth to take her place. He grabbed the entire fleshy opening of her cunt with his teeth and gnawed, drawing blood from her tender insides. She moaned and closed her eyes as a smile spread across her face.

Another woman had gotten to his prick. She sat on it and twisted her hips around its rigid shape. She squealed and wildly rolled her eyes. When she had climaxed, others took her place.

They took turns until his prick was no longer serviceable, then they all climbed off. Squatting over him, they covered his face and body with hot, yellow piss, in criticism, perhaps, of his performance.

When they had drenched him, they hoisted him to their shoulders and marched back to his hut. They dumped him onto his sleeping mat, then turned and marched out the door and back to the clearing.

A most interesting evening.

Chapter 16

A tragedy had befallen the Geek.

After the ladies had carried him back to the hut, he started pacing the floor and talking to himself angrily. He was really pissed! No pun intended.

He was ready to murder each and every one of them. He muttered wild things about escape, about getting the hell out of their reach. It was really scary. I knew he could never make it off the island. The Geek can't swim and he's afraid of water anyway, not to mention he's seasick prone.

He paced the floor from one end of the hut to the

other, slamming the fist of one hand into the palm of the other.

He moaned about his lousy lot in life. Some lousy lot! At least he wasn't a pink chicken kidnapped through no fault of his own and dragged to a crummy desert island, and fed low-class barnyard trash, probably for the rest of his life. At least he had a sex life *and* his own mat to sleep on.

After about an hour of this he rushed out the door and ran crashing through the giant bamboo stalks of our island paradise, screaming at full volume. Well, of course it was a stupid thing to do, and woke everybody up. Pretty soon there were lights on all over the camp, but after about fifteen minutes the little dwellings one by one returned to darkness.

As soon as it was light enough to see, the dyke skaggs huddled in the clearing and planned their attack. They gathered pans and plates and anything else that could be beaten upon with a stick and could be trusted to make noise without breaking. After distributing them, the women searched the grounds for sticks. When each had found one, they spread out in a long line through the woods, pounding on their pans and yodeling. After about an hour of combing the bushes and undergrowth, they flushed out the Geek, who in panic fled before them to the edge of the island, out of the woods and onto the beach. There he was grabbed by six of the huskiest and carried bodily, kicking and screaming, back to his hut. They threw him stomach down onto his sleeping mat and tied him securely with stout rope.

"We'll be back!" cackled one of them.

"You haven't heard the last of this!" threatened another. They all muttered in agreement as they walked out.

The outcome of the whole thing was that they decided the Geek was not to be trusted any more and needed a guard. For this position of trust they chose a three-hundred-pound Polynesian, who in her delusions of grandeur thought herself the Blob Princess. Everyone who came near her had to curtsy and address her as "Your Highness" or "Your Majesty," or at least, "Princess." Not only was she fat, but she had warts everywhere.

The most noticeable of course were the ones on her face, especially the big one with the hairs growing out of it beside her eye. It was even worse than the ones growing in a cluster just under her left nostril. Her face probably wouldn't have been as bad if she had combed her hair over her one swollen and partially gnawed away ear. But she didn't. Looking at it reminded me of an eggplant partially run over by a truck. Actually her hair probably wouldn't have covered her ear anyway. The mangy patches of black strands that tried valiantly to cover the dirty gray of her scalp barely kept the large flakes of dandruff entangled and could not hide the fact that she was partially bald. I suppose none of this would have mattered to the Geek, who never was too selective about his women, if it hadn't been for her bad breath. It was the essence of all the worst odors known to man, with a little trenchmouth thrown in for character. Probably most of it was caused by her rather greenish teeth, at least those that hadn't turned black in her mouth.

Next to the warts on her face, the ones on her nipples were the worst. Just underneath the part that hardens and gets pointy when someone sucks on it were large matching warts that made you think at first glance that she was double-titted. As I looked more closely I realized that what I thought were spare nipple tips were really large brown moles.

She untied the Geek and lifted him to her face level with one strong muscular arm. Crunching his body against hers she wedged him sideways in the cleavage of her large ballooning breasts. With her free hand she reached down and grabbed the flaccid dangle between his legs to press and roll it between her fingers and thumb. She stroked the head with the fleshy back of her thumb, slowly, stroke after stroke. As her hand massaged, the blood quickened, filling and hardening the limp organ. When it became stiff, she pulled him out of her cleavage and threw him onto his grass mat. She stood over his prostrate body, one leg on each side. Towering above him, she bent her knees to come closer and kneel upon him. She yanked the flaps of skin between her legs apart and pulled them wide to bear down onto his helpless erection the yawning opening she exposed. As her knees bent closer onto his prone body, the silent hungry mouth of her cunt devoured his penis. The head disappeared into the pouting lips, then the shaft slipped inch by inch inside. When her knees touched the grass mat under his body and her hips rested on her heels, she undulated over him, swaying her spine with snake-like ease. While her torso twisted in its kneeling hula, she reached out to his armpits with her fingernails and raked the skin clear on down to his waist, leaving raised welts on his flesh. Her hips bounced harder on his loins. She grabbed his arms, squeezing the flesh of his biceps between claw-like fingers. In her peak, as the flabby cheeks of her buttocks pounded hard upon him, she thundered out a fart so melodious and rich in tone that it made me nostalgic for the circus band with its booming Sousaphone section. The vibrations lingered in the air long after the sound itself had stopped. Then they too faded away, leaving behind only the rich odor. That didn't leave as quickly, but lingered for an hour, a concentrated reminder of the power within her.

The Geek turned his head, inhaling the air he needed through his mouth. He curled his upper lip in distaste, then tightly pressed it to his lower lip, holding a mouthful of breath imprisoned inside. He pushed the air out of his lungs in a rush, then gasped another load, sealing his lips behind.

"Why are you holding your breath?" asked the Blob Princess.

"I don't like the perfume you're wearing."

"Oh, *we're* not wearing any perfume."

"I know," said the Geek, gasping another mouthful of air.

The hefty woman looked puzzled but said nothing as her hips churned around his prick.

"Not only is she beautiful..." said the Geek, rolling his eyes.

She smiled at him seductively, winked an eye and continued to hump him.

Finally she put the palms of her hands on the floor and pushed herself off his body. Her ass loomed above her head as she straightened her knees. She stood up, still bending at the waist, her legs straddling him. She straightened her back and yawned. She turned and walked to the doorway.

"Nice day," she said.

"I wouldn't know."

"Don't expect any sympathy from us. You brought it on yourself."

"I know. I know. But it was worth a try."

"Only if you like being guarded. We told you it was impossible. Consider yourself privileged though, to get into *Our Royal Highness. We* are usually very careful about whom *we* fuck, but in *your* case, *we* are extending charity."

She turned to face him again. Lowering her head she rolled her shoulders as she slithered toward him, extending one foot prissily in front of the other. She stood by his head, leaned over him and pressed her lips firmly onto his, flexing the tiny muscles into and around his mouth. She pushed her tongue between his teeth. She explored his molars, the gaping space where one of them had been pulled, to come to rest finally on a wisdom tooth. She licked his tongue with hers, then tickled the roof of his mouth, stroking the bony palate before reaching the soft flesh behind it.

As she probed deep in his throat, he began to cough and gag.

"What's the matter?" she asked haughtily.

"Too far down. It's like sticking your thumb in when you want to…"

"Are you suggesting that *our* tongue makes you vomit?" she asked in tones of outraged royalty.

"No more than my thumb."

"How *dare* you ? Peasant!"

"Actually, it's kind of easy, Fatso!"

"Fatso! You will address me as Your Highness, or *we* shall kick the shit out of you. Is that clear?"

The Geek studied the massive weight and volume of the Blob Princess, appraising the damage she could do, and replied:

"Yes, Your Highness."

"That's better. Now for coming to your senses you shall have an honor that has been bestowed on no mere man before you." With those words she stood behind the Geek's head on his sleeping mat and squatted over his face to place her cunt directly on his mouth. The cheeks of her ass squeezed his nose as she sat on him. She shimmied and her lumpy flab shook, slapping against his face. The Geek must have known what he was to do for she settled onto him with a contented sigh. The muscles of his throat and jaw rippled as he darted his tongue in and out of her cunt, pressing firmly against her clit and the sides of her slimy Blob Princess vagina.

Perhaps it was some pollen floating in the air. Perhaps it was something in the body of the princess herself. For some reason, at that precise moment the Geek sneezed. His head, imprisoned under the weight of the large woman, jerked upward pushing his nose deep into her rectum. His mouth, covering her cunt, released a spray of germ-laden droplets into her, splattering her inner thighs. He sneezed twice more.

The Blob Princess lurched forward from the force of his movement, and with arms flailing to regain balance, fell flat on his stomach. The side of her head landed on his soft exposed balls. He screamed. She lifted her head, turned and looked down at what she had hit. Shrugging, she slid her hand to them and grasped the tender sac in her palm. She massaged, gently drawing her fingers around it to release then press. She put her lips to the purple flesh, stroking in a continuous circular motion. She lifted her lips and her tongue remained pushed against him. It too moved with a circular motion to caress daintily the puckered flesh. She lapped the entire scrotum delicately, leaving its entire surface glistening and wet.

His prick slowly pushed outward, gaining strength. It grew long and hard. She slipped it between her pressed lips and sucked on it. She ran her tongue down its length. Her jaw worked around it in a circular motion and her teeth chewed. Her cheeks hollowed their insides to press against the sides of his penis and massage the thin skin with their slimy wetness. Her jaw chewed faster as she clutched at the base of his prick. With her fist clenched firmly she licked it with short, even strokes. Her mouth, covering the head of his penis, continued to suck and draw out the liquid that was rising from its base. It spurted out into her waiting mouth. Her head bobbed as she swallowed. White ooze dribbled out of her mouth and mixed with the saliva running down her chin. It dripped off onto the Geek's stomach.

She rolled off his body and sat on the floor beside him. She looked around blankly then stood up and waddled over to the small doorway to sit in it, completely blocking the entrance. She closed her eyes and rested head on chins. Soon she was snoring peacefully. The Geek, seeing that his only exit was blocked, shrugged and fell asleep.

Chapter 17

Invitations had been sent out to the Gaylord
Sunshine and Health Spa. It was to be a special
event in honor of the Sunshine Sappho's new acqui-
sition, the Geek. Excitement was in the air.
Preparations were being made all over the island.
Pink and orange Japanese lanterns were attached
to branches of trees surrounding the clearing and
phosphorescent crepe paper streamers laced from
branch to branch.

Arrangements of *What's New Pussycat?* and the
soundtrack to *Kitten With a Whip* were pulled out

of hiding and dusted off. For the entire day, music was played and amplified, getting everyone into the spirit of the thing.

A meeting was held to discuss the Geek and what could be done with him in the light of his recent escape attempt. He had to be kept docile or he might spoil the party. Angelfood suggested that it might be groovy to let the Geek run free and turn the party into a Geek-hunt. The suggestion was vetoed in favor of Big Maria's idea to tie the Geek as usual to the pole, and after he performed, to tie his arms as well, then forget about him until the party was over. This idea was promptly accepted as being the easiest and most practical. Around three in the afternoon the ladies retired to their huts to get into costume and await their guests from the Gaylord Sunshine and Health Spa.

As the shadows grew longer and the sunlight mellow gold, a few of the women left their huts dressed in high drag.

Sadie the sadist emerged wearing a red leather jockstrap artificially filled with foam rubber. Over her chest she wore a billow-sleeved Tom Jones shirt open clear to the waist where it was tied into a knot. Onto the exposed part of her chest she had pasted wispy balls of artificial hair. She carried a whip and took delight in snapping it at flies and other nudists.

A few minutes later, Mona the masochist

emerged from her hut, wearing only a codpiece and necktie. She had no need to disguise her figure, being slender and small-breasted.

Sadie spotted her.

"Come here, you!" she ordered in a booming voice.

Mona cringed and shrank from her.

"I said come here!"

Mona shuffled to her dejectedly.

"I want to test my new whip," said Sadie. "Turn around." Mona's eyes filled with tears and her lower lip quivered.

"I said *turn around!*"

Mona bowed her head and turned her back to the sadist. Her eyes were wide and her body was tense as she braced herself for Sadie's attack.

The sadist twirled the whip over her head like a lasso. The movement of the leather cutting through the atmosphere in a circle caused the air to sing. The tone grew more and more high-pitched as she drew the whip faster around her head. She slammed down upon the girl's back with a smacking sound of leather cutting flesh, and jerked it away as the girl screamed. She laughed and slashed it down onto her buttocks to leave behind a dark raised welt. Mona fell to her knees sobbing as the whip slashed down a third time, its mark crossing both welts in a long diagonal stroke.

She rolled around in the sand pulling her legs up to her body. She ripped off the codpiece. Flinging it aside, she shoved the fingers of one hand in her cunt and squeezed its flesh against the thumb. The top of her hand rose and fell as the strength of her entire arm pushed her fingers deeper inside. She rolled from side to side, moaning. Her legs, bent at the knees, spread apart and the soles of her feet on the ground supported her weight.

Her mouth open, she lay moaning and gasped for breath. Sweat from her forehead rolled down her face and into her mouth. Her short hair was plastered to her usually pale skin. Her skin was now bright red.

Her hand, deep within her body, shoved harder and squeezed urgently. Her back lurched off the ground and her legs kicked convulsively. She doubled up over the hand still embedded in her body and fell to her side in a fetal position, gasping for breath.

Sadie stood over her, grinning.

"Go back inside and re-do your costume. You look like hell."

When Mona had recovered enough to stand up she grabbed her codpiece and ran into the hut sobbing.

"Crybaby!" muttered Sadie.

Chapter 18

Glowing spots of pink and orange lit the island, silhouetted by the glowing streamers. Males dressed as females danced with females dressed as males and both giggled at the game.

Angelfood, dressed in a lightweight seersucker sports jacket and tight leatherette pants, danced with a blond, hair teased into a high bouffant flip and wearing a black sequined evening gown. They discussed the pros and cons of interracial sex.

"Well, I have nothing against it personally..." he said, flicking his wrist. His hands fell limply, leaving only his little finger raised in a curlicue. "But it's so hard on the children."

"Only if you have them," shrugged Angelfood.

Near the punch table, Mona, looking fresh as new, was smiling at one of the Gaylord campers. He was costumed in a brass D-cup brassiere, obviously stolen from some Wagnerian costume department. On his head was an antlered helmet which he wore over a long blonde wig. Pulled tightly around his waist was a black leather corset and falling from it, a floor-length skirt. Wrapped around his wrist was a length of chain. It hung down to the floor and whipped about wildly whenever he moved his arm to gesture.

"Oh I think it's marvelous that you sing opera!" wailed Mona in her thin, high-pitched voice.

"Yes, I am one of the few sopranos of my kind left in the world," he said in mellow treble overtones. "The art of castration has degenerated tragically since its height in Renaissance Italy. There were many with my kind of voice back then...if you wish, we can go off away from the peasants and I shall sing for you the strains of 'Senta's Ballad' or the passages depicting the cries of the War Maidens. Would you like that, little one?"

Having no desire to be uplifted, I hopped on, scooting under the table to avoid being stepped on. I saw the polished wingtips and black silk pants of the hair fetishist. Next to her stood a guest in rhinestone sandals and an electric pink gown with a slit skirt. I came out of hiding to get a better look. It was strapless. Attached to it was a matching pink ostrich feather boa that trailed to the hem. His hair was black and swept up into a high crowning peak of curls at the top of his head. Dangling from his ears were long earrings, with rhinestones to match his sandals. He was standing with one hip higher than the other, hand resting on one, and looked seductively at the woman he was talking to.

"And what did you say your name was, handsome?" he smiled and winked at her.

"I didn't..." said the fetishist. "But it's Harriet."

"Handsome Harriet."

"What's yours?"

"My friends call me Toodles."

Across the clearing, the Blob Princess, costumed in the robes of a Rinasi master was demonstrating her ability in basic karate to a hefty man dressed as the Blob Princess.

She crashed the side of her hand down onto the seat plank of a picnic table and smashed the wood, leaving a gaping break in the middle.

"Can you do that?" she asked triumphantly.

"Hell yes!" he said as he walked around to the other side. He raised his open hand above his head and slammed it onto the other plank seat. He sent splinters flying as he demolished it.

"Big deal!" scoffed the Blob Princess. "Can you Indian wrestle?

"Of course I can Indian wrestle!"

"I challenge you to a duel!"

"I accept!"

They walked to an undemolished picnic table and sat across from each other. They planted their elbows firmly in the middle on the rough wooden surface and clasped one another's hands, grabbing tightly. The Blob Princess counted to three and the match began. As each strained, face turning red, their arms remained upright, stiffly pushing against one another. Although both were shaking from the strain, neither gave way.

I hopped back to the food table. Maria, dressed as a sailor, was pouring a second glass of punch. She walked over to the Geek, tied securely to the pole and lifted one of the glasses to his lips. When he drained it, she pulled a cookie out of her pocket and offered it to him. He shook his head. She shrugged and walked away.

The lights dimmed. Someone shouted for the Geek to be untied. Maria freed his arms. It was show time so I hopped over to the Geek's feet and waited. Maria bent down and grabbed me.

"Nice chicken," she said to me. "You are really well trained, aren't you?"

She lifted me off the ground and placed me in

the Geek's hands. With his usual showmanship, he lifted me melodramatically high above his head, held me there dangling head down, then slowly lowered me toward his open mouth. I did my part, twisting and flapping my wings, and squawked at the top of my lungs in faked panic as his mouth came closer and closer. Teamwork is an important part of any act and I didn't want to blow it for him by becoming blasé. Once my head brushed past his teeth, however, I became motionless. Now that he couldn't swallow castor oil it was especially dangerous to move or even twitch. I didn't want a repeat of what happened the day of the Great Hard-On. I was still having nightmares about that.

Well, he left me in for the count of three, then slowly pulled me out. He flung his arm aside with me still dangling from his hand and held me there during the applause. When it died, he turned his hand so that I stood upward, still held by my feet. He opened his fist to release me. I flapped down to solid ground, crowing and squawking in fake indignation.

It had been a good show.

By now I was hungry, roaring hungry. I knew I would get fed no more that night so I decided to take things into my own claws. I hopped furtively over to the long table on which the bowls of punch and plates of cookies were sitting. Nobody was there, or seemed to be noticing, being all sexually aroused and into playing heterosexual, so the table was deserted. After making sure that no one was looking, I flapped up onto it and gorged myself on cookie crumbs. The cherry flavored shortbreads were my favorite, crumbling delightfully between my beak. I tried a loose chocolate chip but it melted and ran down my breast feathers smearing the outsides of my beak. I decided chocolate was more trouble than it was worth.

One punchbowl was full. I hopped to the rim and bent over to drink some. A curious taste mixed with the fruit juices seemed to evaporate in my beak. I supposed that all the empty vodka bottles I saw earlier in the trash had some connection. It was tasty, however, and I bent down to have another beakfull.

After a few more swallows, I still wasn't feeling a thing and decided that what I had heard about vodka was a myth. Either a myth or else it didn't affect chickens. I ate a few more cookie crumbs but found my appetite if anything was bigger than before. I gorged down some more cookie crumbs and went back to attack the punch. I perched on the edge to sip and got a lemon fiber in my beak.

I began to feel slightly dizzy and teetered on the slippery glass. I caught my balance but as the table revolved around me I fell backward. By flapping my wings I managed to land feet first on the table. I felt good, and when I crowed, my sound boomed out over the strains of *What's New Pussycat?* that was playing loudly on the portable stereo.

I strutted around the cookie plate, blinking to keep it in focus. I decided it must be moving because I tripped on it and kept falling into the cookies. I landed beak down on a butter macaroon. I nibbled at a crumb but found I wasn't at all hungry any more, and in fact felt quite nauseated. I pushed myself off the plate and strutted through the debris of napkins back to the punch bowl. I was ready for some more. This stuff could really grow on you. I decided not to risk balancing on the edge again. I could reach in by craning my neck over the top. I stretched over the ridge of glass. It felt as if its hardness would cut off my circulation. With my neck bent as far as it would go, and my head as close to the liquid as it would reach, I opened my beak wide and scooped out a load. Straightening my neck, I let it slide down my throat. It was cool, and at the same time burning. The sweet cherry flavor lingered in my mouth while my stomach grew hot.

Things spun faster. The pink and orange of the Japanese lanterns glowed, burned, glistened like throbbing nerve ends. The night became a pink and orange haze.

I felt filled with power. I could do no wrong. I crowed defiantly at the entire bunch of them. I was Superchicken! I leaped to the top of the bowl in a single bound! It was slipperier than I imagined and I found myself teetering back and forth trying to grasp the slippery sides with my mighty claws. I flapped my thunderous wings feeling confident that they would keep me from harm. I toppled forward. The red liquid below me loomed closer. I squawked, amazed that this could be happening to me. Superchicken! The wet surface came up and hit me. The splash went in all directions as I sank into the cherry-flavored pool. I was submerged. I fought my way to the surface and to air. Looking over the cut-glass rim of the bowl I gasped for breath and flapped my wings. They were soaked. All my feathers were soaked. I was soaked.

I grasped for footing but found none on the slippery bottom of the bowl. I slid, landing on my tail. Kicking against the sides, I regained balance. I threw myself forward, flapping. The bowl tipped and I went with it as it landed on its side. The punch and I together rolled out of it, head over tail onto relatively dry land. I hopped unsteadily to the edge of the table and jumped off. I landed hard on my claws and rolled in the sand until I came to a stop. I lay still for a few minutes, letting the ground around me reel.

Soon curiosity got the best of me. I struggled to my feet and hopped rather unsteadily over to the shadowy couple I saw lying on the ground a few feet from the table.

When my eyes focused I saw that it was Harriet and Toodles. Toodles had wrapped his feather boa around Harriet, around her waist, then pulled it down between her legs. With the fluffy end in his hand he was tickling her clit, which he had exposed by spreading the flaps of skin that protected it open with the thumb and index finger of his hand. With the boa in his other hand he stroked her sensitive part, teasing it with the fluttery delicate feathers. She crooned, licking her teeth with her tongue and smiled.

He stroked her inner thighs with the puffy cluster of feathers. She spread her legs wider, stretched her back and laughed in delight.

"Oh…" she gasped, panting. "That's almost as good as hair. Oh…do it again!"

She lay motionless, limp, as he stroked her stomach with the boa, running it upward to her breasts. He lingered on her nipples, flickering the feathers across them, until the tips became hard and pointed.

Her clothes were in a pile beside her head, along with the gown worn by Toodles, now dressed only in a black lace garter belt, net stockings and his rhinestone sandals. He wasn't wearing any panties, and his prick hung down past the lace rosettes of his garters.

He ran the very tip of the boa in the convolution of Harriet's ear, then over the outer edge to the part of her neck just below and behind it. She moaned ecstatically and slipped her hands down under Toodles' body and between her own legs. It disappeared. Her arm thrust forward, pushing. Her legs spread even wider and I saw only the top of her hand close against her body, her fingers swallowed up into her cunt. She thrust and released, bringing them partially out, covered with slime. She would push them back up into her again, squeeze, then pull them out again as far as her middle knuckles. She churned her insides continuously as Toodles tickled her body with the feather boa.

The soft dangle of skin between Toodles' legs began to twitch, reluctantly, weakly. He crawled up beside Harriet's head. Leaning over to balance on the palms of his hands, he lifted one leg over her head and kneeled, his prick dangling over her mouth.

"Lower it! I can't quite reach it."

He kneeled lower, and the head of his penis lay like a dead weight on her lips. She opened her mouth and it fell inside between her teeth. He lowered himself and it rested against the back of her tongue. She curled her tongue around and delicately licked the shaft below the head with the tip. She closed her lips around it and sucked. Her jaws chewing gingerly, she worked up and down while her tongue inside licked at it. She sucked at him until he came in her. She had never done it before, or didn't like it or something, but as his come surged out into her mouth she coughed and spit it out. I hopped on, leaving her with her face covered with the sticky goo.

At the edge of clearing, across the clusters of bodies on the ground and the Geek still tied to his pole, I saw the Blob Princess and her rival still sitting face to face at the wooden picnic table, elbows still pressed to the table top. Their fists were still clenched together and both arms completely upright. Both of them were gritting their teeth and staring balefully at each other. The shoulders were hunched forward, muscles knotted.

By now the churning in my stomach was boiling, splashing against the sides of my throat. Becoming more turbulent, it erupted in a molten mass into my craw and out of my beak in massive rushes of quivering half-digested cookie crumbs. My stomach tightened again, forcing it's contents out. It tightened again and completely emptied itself of any hidden traces of food and booze that may have been clinging to its lining. My stomach contracted again and a thin, watery liquid spurted out and onto the pile of sludge, soaking into the ground in front of me. It tightened again and nothing came out. All the muscles of my stomach and throat forced themselves out toward my mouth. My whole body pushed forward to empty my already empty stomach. I nearly fell on my beak into the puddle of vomit in front of me. My head was reeling. I nearly fell on my side as I hopped rather unsteadily toward Roxie the Recreation Director and her leather freak drag-queen companion.

He was dangling upside down by his knees from the sturdy low, hanging limb of an avocado tree. As he hung with blood rushing into his head Roxie stood half stooping in front of him, mouth under the dick dangling against his belly button.

She scooped it into her open mouth and grabbed the base near his balls with her hand, milking it like a cow teat, ready to catch and swallow his sperm when it shot out of him. With her other hand she gently squeezed and released the sperm sac, goading it and bringing his organ to a pitch of rigid excitement. She sucked harder and her hand pulled and gripped more tightly on his erect penis as her cheeks pressed themselves around the head inside her mouth. The movement of her hands slowed but kept a forceful, even rhythm toward her face. The organ bobbed under her fingers and she began to swallow furiously. Her arms fell limp to her side. She stopped swallowing and stepped back to straighten up.

Still hanging, he grabbed the tips of her boobs in both hands and pinched them. He rolled the brownish tips between his fingers and the balls of his thumbs, and they became stiff and hot. He cupped his hand under one shiny, well-filled breast and kneaded it while his fingertips explored the mysteries of her cleavage. With his hand firmly gripping her breast he pulled her to him and took it in his mouth. He sucked like a baby boy, smacking his lips against her with relish.

She cradled her hand under the top of his head as if to hold him up in case his knees straighten and he should fall head first from the green leafy branch.

Instead, an avocado dropped from on high and landed, splattering its soft ripe insides all over her skull. The pit rolled out, bounced off her shoulder and landed on the sandy ground beneath her feet.

"Goddamn it!" said Roxie.

"It kind of spoils the mood," said the naked leather freak dangling from the avocado branch.

"I have a headache already," she muttered.

. He grabbed the branch with his hands and pushed his knees away from it, tucking them under and then dropping down. He dangled by his hands for a few seconds before letting go, swinging back and forth, then dropped to the ground with a thud.

A piece of avocado had landed near me but I don't like avocado meat so I hopped away to watch the action as Sadie stuck heated pins into the quivering ass of a fat, whimpering boy crouched over in a fetal position on the ground.

She stood behind him, legs spread far apart, with one hand on her hip. With the other she reached toward the small bonfire she had built to one side and pulled from it a glowing, red-hot hatpin. Holding it gingerly at the tip she plunged it into the meaty flesh shaking in terror at her feet. She pushed it in slowly, letting the hot steel sear the layers of flesh and fat. He screamed, his voice rising to a high pitch like an infant. As she pushed another glowing pin into his flesh, he grabbed the little boy prick dangling between his fat legs and began to pull on it. He pushed it forward toward the head as the metal shoved deep into his meat, pulling the loose skin back and forth as Sadie reached for yet another pin.

The pulling and pushing motion became faster as Sadie ran out of pins and had to yank out the six that were already embedded but cooling now in his ass. He panted as his chubby hands tightly grasped their treasure. Sweat poured from him at his exertion.

He screamed again as yet another pin was

shoved by the merciless Sadie into his fat little tushie. Soon his efforts were rewarded as spurts of come gushed unevenly out of his little stiff prick.

Sadie threw her leg over his back and mounted him. She squirmed, pressing her cunt down onto his backbone, squeezing her legs into his flabby sides. All six hatpins were still sticking from the cheeks of his ass and after she dug her knees into his sides, she slammed her hand down on the pins, forcing them deeper into his fat.

"Ride, ya little cocksucker!" she squalled, slapping his ass again and again. He screamed and tears rolled out of his eyes.

"I said *move!*"

He started forward awkwardly on his hands and knees. She shoved her knees into his sides once more.

"Faster!"

He crawled faster and lost balance, falling over to one side and spilling Sadie.

"Goddamn you clumsy son of a bitch!" she screamed. "I'll whip your ass for that!"

She pulled herself out from under him and stood up.

"Stay where you are, you fat asshole. I'm going to get my whip and if you're not here when I get back, I'll find you and your ass won't be fit to sit on for a month!"

He crouched, a jellied mass of terror, curled tightly, head tucked under his arm and whimpering. He was still crouching with pins in ass when Sadie returned with her whip.

"Stand up!"

He stood expectantly.

"If you were even remotely intelligent, you would have taken the pins out while I was gone. How do you expect me to whip you when the pins get in the way?"

He looked at her questioningly.

"Yes dum-dum, I want you to take them out."

Lethargically he pulled a pin from his ass, looked at it, then looked at her questioningly.

"Give to me," she said in a tone of controlled annoyance, "and hurry up. We only have all night."

He pulled out the others, slowly, methodically, and handed them to her one at a time. When he had pulled the last of them out, she smiled and said sarcastically:

"*Very* good. That took wisdom. Now let's see how well you do at something really complicated like leaning against a tree. I want your back toward me. You'll need support. I'm strong and I'll get annoyed if you lose your balance."

She led him over to a date palm. He extended his arms and leaned against it. She threw the whip behind her, then yanked it forward like a fishing line to slam it against the quivering flesh of his back. Its lash cut into his chubbiness and he screamed as the thong dragged across to reveal a thick purple-red welt. She yanked the whip back over her head once more and slashed it across the flesh of the fat little masochist. It whipped through the air and slammed again on his back. The tender skin soon became covered with the crossed lines from the whip. Blood trickled out of some, beading at the wound itself, then rolling sluggishly down his back.

Sadie flung the whip aside.

"Kneel!"

He obeyed.

"Kiss my feet!"

He bent and placed his lips on her toes, lingered in that position, then straightened.

"Now stand."

He pushed himself up, grunting, huffing and puffing.

"Now kiss my ass!"

He bowed and pressed his mouth onto the cheek of her buttocks.

"Now do ten push-ups!"

He groaned and his jowls quivered. A disconsolate expression turned the corners of his eyes and mouth down. His nostrils enlarged in distaste.

"I said *get down and do the push-ups,* you lazy blob of blubber!"

He lay stomach down on the ground, his hands underneath his chest. He pushed himself up from the ground, stiffening his arms with one mighty effort. He collapsed and fell back limp face down.

"That's one."

He groaned and pushed himself up once more, bending his knees and arching his back.

"You're cheating. You're supposed to keep your legs straight."

He groaned and pushed himself about a foot off the ground before he collapsed. But his legs were straight.

"You know, you are really a pig."

His lip quivered as a woebegone expression crossed his face. He lay limply on his stomach looking too dejected even to move.

"You've only done three," said Sadie sternly, "and I'm being lenient. The last two were pretty shitty push-ups."

He sighed and pushed himself away once more from the ground. He made only a foot's distance then lowered himself, quickly raising his body once then twice again before he collapsed panting in the sand.

"Four more to go," said Sadie, counting on her fingers.

Bending his knees he pushed off again. Sadie lifted another finger to mark his progress. Once again he pushed his body away from the sand. Another finger was raised.

"That makes eight," she said tapping her foot impatiently. "If you don't hurry it up I'll get the whip again."

Panting hoarsely he lifted himself off the ground yet another time, about half the distance of the time before. Sweat poured out of his skin and rolled down his face and back in large droplets.

"That was nine. It also was shitty but I suppose I can't expect miracles. One more and you're through."

He took a deep breath, let it out with a sigh, looking defeated. He paused, took another breath and grunted, pushing himself up. When his chin was about four inches from the ground he collapsed again.

"That's ten. Now let's go over and have some punch and cookies."

I had a chilly feeling in the pit of my craw. I hopped to the edge of the nearby clearing to see what would happen. They walked together to the table. Sadie stood, her hands on her hips, staring at the overturned punchbowl

"What the hell," she exclaimed. "And what..." she continued, looking at the cookie plate.

"What the hell happened here?"

She stared wide-eyed at the debris.

"Feathers!" she roared. "Fucking pink chicken feathers!"

"What's the matter, Sadie?" asked Harriet from the ground at her feet.

"The table's a mess, our booze is spilled, the cookies are all crumbled and there are chicken feathers all over the table and plastered to the sides of the punch bowl. Pink chicken feathers!"

"What the hell?" asked Toodles, forgetting his dainty way of talking.

"That damned pink chicken got into our food!" screamed Harriet.

"What's going on?" asked Roxie.

"Just wait until I get my hands on that damned chicken!" roared Sadie.

I decided it would be most healthy to get out of sight for a while. I furtively hopped out of the clearing past the Blob Princess and her opponent, down the path to the Geek's hut. I found a nice cool corner, settled down and went to sleep for the rest of the night.

Chapter 19

The following morning I was out hopping around looking for hookworms to supplement my diet, when in a distance, across the debris-covered clearing, I saw a vision. A hen so plump, so shiny and so delectable that I couldn't believe my eyes. As she strutted, her little red-brown tail feathers wiggled so seductively that I wanted to flap across the clearing then and there and mount her. I felt my cock harden just looking at her. As I stealthily hopped toward her to get a better look at her plump breast and downy neck, I could feel my cock throb and tighten, pushing out my feathers. A rushing noise filled my ears and my body grew hot, burning hot.

As I approached, she heard and quickly turned to see what the noise was. She was alert too. I liked that in a hen. She regarded me with her shiny eyes, black as tar, and clucked questioningly. Maybe she had never seen another chicken. I hoped not. I wanted to break her in.

I had plans. Big plans. A hen at last! And she was all mine. My breath came in fast rushes. I motioned with my head that we should go off into the woods together. I wanted to get her where it was quiet. I would stand a better chance of getting into her if there was no one around. She clucked and turned her head coyly away at my motion, but I persisted, crowed and beat my wings against my chest. Finally she hopped over beside me, standing close, and together we hopped down the vine-tangled path to the darkest wilderness of the island.

As we bounced along, I became so excited with anticipation that I came in my feathers, getting sticky stuff all over myself. I cursed and began to work on getting it up again. As we hopped, I studied the fine lines of her tail, her tasty plumpness. I tried to imagine me inside her, warmed by her hot little body.

Nothing happened.

My prick, still wet from its premature spilling out, dangled limp and dead between my legs.

I tried to imagine the sight of her gasping in pain as the unaccustomed object was forced into her tender opening. The pain would fade into pleasure and her gasps and tears would turn into those of joy. A shudder would run through her plumpness as I thrust deeper into her, touching parts that she had never known existed before I opened them. My seed would shoot out in a hot spurt inside, slamming against the wall of her womb, to scorch it with my passion. These thoughts came to nothing.

My prick, a little drier, still dangled limply between my legs.

My little dumpling had stopped. Perched on a rock she looked at me expectantly. I was panic-stricken. If I didn't perform well, I might never get another chance. She would look upon me with scorn. I closed my eyes, took a deep breath and tried to concentrate on getting it up. Still my cock hung limp between my legs. My heart beat faster and I had the urge to run away and end it all. The hen, by now impatient, was clucking angrily. I didn't know what to do. I tried to get behind her and rub it against her, in the hope that it might be inspired by such a fine piece of tail.

When she felt that nothing was happening she

hopped away from me. She turned around, looked at me with contempt and clucked in derision. I was never so humiliated! I tried to convince her that it was merely because I was hung over, but she only cackled. It was too much. I felt crushed and wished for a quick death. She turned and hopped away, shaking her tail in my face as she went down the path.

After she had disappeared from sight, my prick, until now limp and soft, began to harden, throbbing erratically as it slowly became stiff, then stiffer. I gritted my beak and saw red! Crowing in angry frustration, I beat my prick wildly against a nearby tree.

Chapter 20

That night after dinner the women tied the Geek to the pole again and someone grabbed me. I was put into his hands to be swallowed. He lifted me high above him and plunged me down his throat. After he pulled me out he let go and settled into a dejected slump, sighing in misery.

"Why me?" he muttered to himself.

I stood at his feet and tried to crow hearteningly. He looked down at me and sighed. He lifted his eyes and stared into space, far above everybody's head. I turned and hopped away, and I hadn't gone

far when I nearly tripped over the body of Harriet,
her face buried in the fuzzy natural hair of
Angelfood, who was lying on Harriet's stomach.
Harriet moaned and nuzzled more deeply into the
pile of hair that covered her face as she wrapped
her legs tightly around the torso of the negress. Her
back arched as she squeezed the bulbous boobs in
her cupped hands. Angelfood moaned and pressed
her cunt toward Harriet. Angelfood reached
between Harriet's spread legs and slid her fingers
into her soft wet opening. Angelfood pressed the
heel of her hand against the bone of Harriet's
pelvis, and pushed her fingers inside the white girl.
When she rolled off Harriet, Angelfood lay back
down on the ground beside her. The hair fetishist
sat up and bent forward to rest her chest on one of
Angelfood's legs. She planted her head between the
strong limbs and covered the opening of the black
girl's cunt with her mouth. Her jaw moved as loud
slurping noises emerged from her lips and tongue
against the wet flowing flesh of her lover.

Angelfood twined her legs around Harriet's neck
and contracted the muscles of her ass, forcing her
body forward against the mouth of the woman
between her legs. Harriet's jaw moved faster as her
teeth bit down, gently nipping the tip of Angelfood's
clitoris. She stretched her mouth open as wide as
her jaws would go, reaching deep into Angelfood's

cunt with her tongue to lick the salty sides of her vagina. She reached, stretching the muscle to explore the dark recesses of her womb, her face plastered against the outer lips of Angelfood's cunt. She pulled away far enough to see her tongue dart quickly in and out. As it licked the tender part hidden inside the pendulous flaps of skin between Angelfood's legs, the negress' muscles tightened and relaxed, pressing against Harriet's body as a low contralto moan escaped from her full lips.

Slowly, while watching them, my own willful dangler was twitching. It hardened and became rigid. Pressure built up inside, pushing against the walls and my penis became swollen. It throbbed urgently as blood pushed harder against the head. I saw a movement out of the corner of my eye. I turned to see what it was, and, to my delight, saw that it was that delectable little hen. Her back was turned. I would sneak up on her and surprise her. I stealthily hopped over to where she stood. Before she knew what hit her, I mounted her from behind and forced my hard prick into the fluffy feather opening under her tail. She was tight. I heard her gasp as it burned its way into her body, searing her flesh as it forced the tender walls of her tiny opening apart by its onslaught.

I pushed deeper and another shuddering gasp escaped from her. I filled the space she had never known existed. My red-hot organ tore into the innermost sanctum of her body, brazenly outraging the dark secret recesses. Her slick flesh pressed against the sides of my cock and eagerly massaged it. The muscles rippled as they held me tightly in her warm, clammy womb. The suction of her insides teased the sperm that filled me up. It rose toward the head, and out with a spurting gush, filling her insides with its volume. She cackled wildly as I pulled myself out, limp and shrunken but feeling GOOD! GOOD! GOOD!

I crowed tenderly at the little birdlet. She was my first!

I nuzzled against her, tickling the side of her head with my comb. She clucked softly and contentedly while she stroked upward against the feathers of my breast with her beak. I was pleased with myself and crowed exultantly.

Behind me I heard a sound halfway between crowing and clucking. I whirled around outraged, ready to kill the intruder if necessary. Several feet away, hopping toward us, tail wiggling from side to side like a hen, was a rooster, large and thin with ruffled feathers and his comb pulled partially back. He crowed again softly, trying to imitate, and partially succeeding, the cackle of a hen. He flapped one wing limply in my direction, raising the tip in a curlicue, and crowed again.

He rushed at the hen flapping both wings and uttering a full rooster crow. He tried to bite out her eyes with his beak. She ducked and he attacked again, flapping on top of her, digging into her back with his claws. She cackled and flapped, throwing him off balance. She turned quickly and imbedded her beak into his exposed wingpit. He crowed in outraged amazement and tried to close his wing over her body to crush her. She pulled out her beak and grabbed his wing inside it, clamping down. He crowed again in pain and tried to flap his wing.

She backed away, charging head down and knocked him off balance. He landed on one wing and she rushed at him again embedding her beak in his side. He flapped his wings and crowed in agony as she jumped up and down on top of him. He lay, his head drooping limply on the ground as she stomped. She cackled triumphantly as he weakly crowed in defeat. I, for one, felt sorry for the strange rooster. She jumped off his body and stood over him, cackling in derision until he struggled to his feet and hobbled away, barely able to keep his balance.

After we had screwed once more she told me about him. He called himself Rita. He was a hen impersonator. Whenever a rooster was on the island, he would battle all available hens for the affections of the rooster.

Actually it seemed reasonable that he should be attracted to me. I am a handsome devil and my coloring is rare.

I was rather proud of the way she put up a fight. It showed spunk, and I liked that in a hen.

I patted her on the tail with my wing and sent her back to the hen house. She was tired and would have to be up early tomorrow to lay her quota of eggs. Besides, I was tired.

After she had disappeared into the hen house I hopped across the clearing to watch the match between the Blob Princess and her rival from across the water. Neither had given an inch. Everyone else from the Gaylord Sunshine and Health Spa had gone back sometime in the middle of last night, leaving him alone to finish his battle. Their lips were drawn tightly back from their gritted teeth. Both breathed heavily. I casually wondered how much longer they could go on without eating or sleeping.

I hopped past them and stood warming myself at Sadie's bonfire. In a specially constructed holder she had four brands heating on the flames. At her feet, bent on her side and tightly bound, was Mona, dear sweet masochistic Mona. She was whimpering and started sobbing when Sadie's foot crashed into her exposed buttocks.

"Wormwench!" bellowed Sadie. "What are you good for?"

Wormwench's sobs wracked her entire being and her movement, inspired by agony, strained her body against the ropes that bound her tightly.

"Whimper and cry. Cry and whimper. You are a sniveling mass of existential futility. You would be better off dead!"

Mona's sobs turned to wails. Sadie kicked her again.

"You've probably never even been laid. You are probably still a virgin! You're so chickenshit you were probably scared to lose it."

Mona's sobs grew louder and became more high-pitched and desperate.

"I'm right—aren't I?"

Mona nodded miserably.

"We'll have to fix that, won't we, you little piece of wormy apple!"

Mona cringed in terror.

"No, please," whimpered Mona, "I'm not ready. Please!"

"Well I'm not going to do it tonight," said Sadie caustically. "Tonight I'm going to brand you. I've other plans for the Cherry Popping Festival."

"What do you mean?"

"I have to make plans. I want it to be an event that will go down in the history of the island."

"No, please!"

"Don't talk back!" growled Sadie as she pulled a

glowing brand from the fire. She stared at the target, held the heated metal above her head to plunge it torrero-style into the plump rounded protuberances of Mona's buttocks. The girl screamed shrilly as the heated metal seared a design into her flesh. Sadie pulled it off. Around the red mark left by the brand rose whisps of smoke. Mona groaned softly and continuously as she heard Sadie pull another brand from the fire. She shrieked as its glowing tip sizzled into her meat.

"That's enough of that!" said the sadist. "If I get carried away now, you won't have any room left for later and I won't be able to fry your hide any more."

She kicked the bound girl over on her back. Her arms and legs, all tied together, were stuck over her head, while her cunt (unprotected by her legs) lay exposed to Sadie's view. The sadist kneeled in front of it and viciously jammed three fingers into the lubricated opening. Mona screamed as the woman's fingernails cut into her flesh and scraped her insides. Pressing from within, against her thumb, Sadie squeezed with all her strength, gritting her teeth. Mona begged her to stop. Sadie paused, then pulled her hand from Mona's vagina.

"You're right. I don't want to deflower you just yet. Thank you for reminding me, dear. And now, little piss pot, let me untie you. I want you to get a good night's sleep, or several good nights' sleep, so that you will be fresh for the big day. Go to bed."

Mona trudged dejectedly away to her hut, as Sadie carefully set her brands aside to cool.

Nearby, at the pole, the Geek was straining to untie the knots that bound him. Since most of them were tied from behind he was having difficulty. He sighed, stopped, and looked with disgust at the dykes who were whipping and masturbating each other. He snarled and fought with the ropes once more. Again he failed to undo the tightly pulled knots.

"Hey!"

No one paid attention to him.

"Hey! Someone untie me!"

No one listened. He cursed angrily.

"God fuck it! Someone cut me loose! It won't kill you! I can't escape!"

Roxie stood up with a sigh.

"All right, all right! I'm coming! Keep your pants on!"

She went behind him and untied the knots.

"Now shut up and go to sleep or something. And if you're smart you won't try another escape thing."

"So all right. I know better! I just want to get some sleep, that's all."

"So good night."

Chapter 21

"Goddamn it, Hilda's been laying nothing but fertilized eggs for the whole damn week! All the girls have been bitching and you can't blame them. Who wants to eat fertilized eggs?"

"Not to mention that you have to eat them right away, or else refrigerate them, if you don't want to end up trying to scramble a chicken fetus."

"Since we don't have an icebox, that's a real problem."

"I didn't think that rooster we have was any good for that sort of thing."

"He's not. It's that damn pink chicken. He's been fucking Hilda every chance he gets. Whenever we're doing it and she's roaming around, he'll be there with his cock stuck in her."

"Thinks he's human?"

"How the hell should I know? I never see him do it when none of us are doing it though."

"It's kind of cute."

"Not when you have to eat fertilized eggs it isn't."

She broke yet another of Hilda's lovely eggs into the pan, scrambling it with the fork she was holding. She beat it by scraping the fork against the side of the pan.

"I think we'll have to lock Hilda in the hen house or something."

"Either that or tie up the stupid pink chicken."

"It's easier to pen up the hen. Anyway she sometimes lays her eggs in strange places. This way they'll all be together."

I hopped out of the way of her feet. She looked down and scowled.

"Oh shit! There's that damned chicken again. Underfoot as usual. I nearly stepped on him."

She clapped her hands and stared toward me.

"Shoo! Shoo! Go on! Get out! Shoo!" She ran toward me as I flapped toward the edge of the clearing. "Scram!"

I crowed in protest as I headed for the shelter of the woods. First they were destroying the lovely eggs I had so blissfully fertilized, and then they were going to keep me from my beloved Hilda, and now this, to be driven away like a common nuisance. It was really too much.

About ten yards away I saw Rita the Rooster cackle—crowing triumphantly at the news of Hilda's confinement. I felt like biting and tearing off his comb, but I knew he would be overjoyed if I did.

I hopped off in a huff.

Chapter 22

After a long dry week, I decided in desperation to give the dainty Mr. Rita a try.

As he stood at the edge of the clearing about ten feet from me, I winked at him. His eyes glazed over in surprise, and he cackled questioningly. I winked again and crowed enticingly.

His eyes brightened in eager anticipation and he hopped toward me hesitatingly. I flapped my wings and crowed again. Rita came close and turned his back on me and I climbed on. I jammed my sex-starved cock up his ass. His opening was smaller than Hilda's cunt, and dry, but the muscles that lined the walls of his anus gripped me tightly, pressing into the sides of my cock. It was satisfying enough to let me forget, at least for the time being, my darling Hilda. Actually I rather enjoyed the change and wondered casually if I too might not be a little peculiar. I didn't worry about it a great deal as I pumped into the body of my rooster lover, but it nagged at my brain just a little. What actually bothered me was the thought that this method of lovemaking might be unhealthy. The strain of the cock stretching the muscles of the large intestine might in time cause hemorrhoids.

Hemorrhoids are not nice things to have. I know. My grandmother had hemorrhoids in her later years, before they wrung her neck and boiled her for soup.

For that reason I was a little doubtful about letting Rita do it to me in the same way. I figured his hemorrhoids were his own business but I didn't want any. I refused to let him touch me. He took it quite well and seemed good-natured about it. Actually I think he preferred the passive role anyway.

Chapter 23

When Roxie cut the Geek loose the other night, he went straight back to his hut and fell asleep. The following dawn, when they came to check on him, he was still there, snoring peacefully. Seeing him restored their confidence.

From then on he was allowed to roam unguarded. During the days he was free to do whatever he pleased. Only his nights were occupied with entertaining the campers. He seemed satisfied with the arrangement and gave the sapphists no trouble.

Actually, if they knew how he was spending his

days, they would feel less than secure about him. While the sun blazed away he would lose himself in the woods, collecting piles of driftwood, palm fronds, and avocado branches. He would tie them together with vines and hide them under shrubbery and piles of rock, marking the spots with wet branches. Actually he didn't have any difficulty since most of them were hidden in the same general location and were easy to find. It was impossible to tell from looking at the Geek that he had any plans of that sort. He acted so cheerful and casual around his captors that none of them ever suspected. Even I, knowing the Geek as well as I do, would never have known, if one day I hadn't been out hopping around in the underbrush looking for Rita who was at the time playing hard to get. I ran into one of the piles he had stashed away. Lashed together with some twine he had found in the woods were about six sturdy avocado branches.

I heard footsteps and stayed where I was, hidden under the bush. Soon, as the crackling of feet crushing twigs became louder, the form of the Geek appeared, with a large bundle of palm fronds in his arms. He threw them on the ground and pulled a length of wild grape vine from around his neck. He wrapped it around the palm fronds and stuck the tied bundle under the edge of the bush where I was hiding.

I hopped to a more comfortable hiding place

behind a large rock. In about half an hour he returned with a large bamboo stalk that had broken off at the ground and threw that too onto the wild grass patch that formed a natural clearing in the heart of the woods.

This was beginning to be interesting.

I forgot all about Rita as I settled down to watch how this strange activity would shape up.

The Geek was smiling as he cheerfully hummed the tune of "Don't Fence Me In."

He arranged a pile of small rocks around the bush that sheltered the pieces of wood and bamboo, then burst into a tuneless chorus of "Sailing, Sailing, Over the Bounding Main."

I surmised from this that he had escape on his mind. This was getting more interesting by the minute.

As I watched, he went out and brought back several more stalks that he had gathered.

When the sun had fallen to the horizon and streaks of orange and red colored the sky, the Geek sighed and went down to the nearby beach. He walked a few yards out into the breakers until his body had been completely soaked, then walked back through the wooded wilderness down the path to the clearing.

I spent my afternoons from then on watching the Geek.

After about a week he had begun to tie sections of wood or bamboo together with the thick vines that grew wild on the island. He would lash the vines under then over the branches, then weave the vines back in the other direction. His progress was slow, but still he worked on with determination.

About three days a week he would spend lolling around in his hut to avoid any suspicion. His captors would sometimes come to visit and chat with him, little suspecting that he had any plans.

I decided to stick close by the Geek, so that when he was ready to leave, I would leave with him. By now I was sick unto death of Rita, and wanted to get into a hen again. Oh, not that Rita wasn't delightful in his own way, but just how much rooster can any other rooster take? It was getting to be a drag.

Chapter 24

It was quiet this morning. So quiet that the silence hung heavily around me. It was the kind of breathless silence that almost makes you afraid to crow. It was a very peculiar day, with the electrical stillness of a storm about to break. Patches of cloud hung in the sky, a glowing gray, tinted by the peculiar shade of blue that colored the sky, and lit by the sun whose rays were choked off behind them.

Despite the lateness of the hour, no one was up. I probably should have crowed but I decided not to.

It seemed only fair after the great entertainment of last night.

It was an evening dear little Hilda would have loved. Too bad about her. Such a dumpling she was, and a great lay once she had caught on to the whole thing. She was a good sport too. And talk about a fighter! I'll never forget the way she wiped out that fag rooster if I live to be ten!

Last night was Mona's cherry popping. It was too beautiful! There she was, all glowing and innocent, her little cherry just aching to be popped. Too bad she wasn't a chicken. The things I could do to her! Just thinking about it makes my beak drip!

They brought her out on a wagon, all shy and modest, bound like a sacrifice. The older dykes surrounded her to keep her on balance as the wagon jolted. Glistening in the moonlight, she was naked except for the bouquet in her cunt—three white roses stuck up her snatch. Only the heads showed. She had to keep her legs spread in order not to crush them. Her pubic hair had been shaved. Pasted onto the freshly exposed skin were lilies of the valley and wild daisies.

When the wagon stopped they lifted her out and carried her to a makeshift altar. Talk about losing your virginity in style! They lifted her up and tied her hands to an overhanging branch, her ankles to hooks at the sides.

Around the altar were lighted torches. In front of her was one bayberry-scented candle held in a carved wooden holder.

Sadie stood behind her with a pigskin whip. She whirled it then slammed it down on the girl's bare ass. She squirmed, screaming as it landed on her skin. The way she moaned and smiled I could tell she loved it. She writhed in pleasure as the dyke sadist let out a karate yell and brought the leather thong curling over her shoulder to cut into the girl's left boob. Glistening perspiration rolled from her armpits, down the sides of her body to drip into the roses. As her body jerked away from the force of the whip, she licked her lips, salty from the sweat that poured down her face. She moaned. The growing moisture from her cunt was beginning to dislodge the roses, while her hips, as if to help the flowers along, were twitching in even rhythm to the black leather whip.

I must be a dyed-in-the-feathers fetishist. Those flowers really turned me on, and as I watched, my little cock grew harder and harder. I was looking around for something to relieve myself on, when up swished Rita the Rooster.

Lovely Rita...Rooster Man...Where would I be without him?

Rita was looking lovelier than ever. He had somehow managed to tape down his comb and easily passed as a hen. As he sneaked up behind me he managed a very hen-like cluck. I whirled around in a heat, thinking Hilda had escaped and was ready to rape her on the spot. I was bitterly disappointed when I saw him. I made the best of it, however. I let him take my cock within his beak. It wasn't too bad, although not at all what I was in the mood for. I could have preferred the warm cunt of a hen to the beak of a rooster any day. Sex with Rita wasn't bad though. He sucked and chewed vigorously, drawing the sap of my ever-hardening prick closer to the top, then out into his mouth. As he swallowed I began to take less of a dim view of the whole matter.

By now they were branding Mona. Sadie pulled the glowing iron from the fire and planted it sizzling on her tender flesh. She screamed, tears rolling from her eyes as she twisted in agony. Her tormentor pressed the iron against the inside of her leg, up near the roses, now wilted, that hung halfway outside of her vagina. The sadist pulled the iron off, revealing a bright red mark. Sticking the brand into the flames again, she left it until it glowed white hot. She pulled the metal out of the fire, carefully lowering the burning metal to the plump meat of the virgin's buttocks. As she screamed, I heard sizzling. The girl's body writhed, twisting against the ropes that bound her. Hips gyrating, she flung the roses out of her cunt into the audience of those who had come to watch the entertainment, while their fingers were inserted in their own vaginas.

One of the ladies was reminded of her youth when a dripping rose hit her cheek, and commented on the similarity of events in her past.

"Reminds me of a strip act I once caught in Toledo. This dame, Mum la Mum I think her name was, after she goes as far as she can with her peeling, she takes and sticks a mum up her cunt, pulls it out and zaps it at some dirty old man in the audience. You know, one of those that wears his hat out on his lap then stands up and the hat is still hanging on?

"Well the time I saw the act it was with some straight guy I picked up for free drinks. Mumsie tossed out the flower and it went splat right across my date's mouth. Well he jumped up, leaned over and puked right there on the floor all over everything. Funnier 'n shit!"

"I heard about that act," replied Cleo, standing at her side, all the fingers of her right hand in her cunt. "Mum la Mum is kind of famous. Whatever happened to her, anyway?"

"Well the last I heard, Toledo was trying to outlaw her place by putting a ban on burlesque."

"How come?"

"Well it all started about three months earlier. Well, you heard about Toledo. It used to be called the drag capitol of the nation, even beating Fire Island. Anyway, there was this big raid on a whorehouse there, probably an independent one, they never touch the ones owned by the Church or organized crime. Probably this guy didn't pay dues to the cops or something. Well anyway, they rounded up all the girls and got them to the station. Imagine their surprise when they found out that about half of the girls were boys. Of course no one was surprised but the politicians. They acted very righteous, made speeches blaming the poor fags for Toledo's rising crime rate and increased violence, as well as everything else lousy with the city. And there was plenty! Council passed laws making it illegal, immoral, and fattening to be gay. After that, they started passing all kinds of laws against vice, sin, and evil, to show the taxpayers that they were zealously guarding the welfare of the city. After outlawing the evil of going in drag, they tried to outlaw evil burlesque, a move especially aimed at Mum la Mum who was planning to move her place into the business district, upsetting the directors of some girlie charm school located down the block."

"Oh how delightful!" laughed Cleo as she licked her dripping fingers. "What happened then?"

"The high school kids who lived there could

never understand why the men who supposedly ran the city had never heard about Toledo's status in the underground. Since they had known about it for years, it seemed incredible that their fathers could miss the meaning of certain advertisements on the radio like the one for *The Gay Kittycat,* an ad for a bar-nightclub singing the praises of the exotic Mr. Rhonda and the beautiful Mr. Shalambo seemed pretty obvious to the kids, but then high school students are not naive.

"The pity of it is, the only thing that made Toledo interesting were its vices and drag queens, and after they outlawed them, the town had nothing to offer!"

"What happened to burlesque in Toledo after that?" asked her companion.

"Mum fought. As far as I know, she won. The law was unconstitutional. That never bothered Toledo City Council before, but Mum had the money to fight back."

"Sounds like a good place to leave!" said Cleo.

"That's about what it's good for!" said the woman.

Up on the altar, Roxie cut the virgin down and lowered her now-limp body onto the floor. I kind of wondered where they were going from there. The Geek was the only man on the island, and I didn't think they would use him. What was left didn't leave much in the way of a choice. I presumed they were going to use a dildo, but that seemed rather mundane. I settled down to watch with interest.

Foreplay accomplished, she was hot and ready, waiting to be penetrated. The dykes encircled her. The oldest pulled a pitch pipe out of her cunt and blew A flat. They hummed the tone in unison and burst into song. Singing, they folkdanced in a circle, hand in hand around her prostrate body. After they had finished, all of them except for Sadie climbed down again and stood on the ground, still surrounding Mona from below. The leader gently pulled the girl's legs apart and while caressing her dripping cunt, reached for the long bayberry candle in the holder.

She lifted it out, and bringing it down, gently inserted the unlit end into the virgin's cunt. Massaging her stomach, and the shaven pubic region, she shoved it deeper and deeper into her, sweating as she thrust the paraffin prick deep into the maidenhead of the young masochist.

The spear disappeared as the head of flame inched closer to the flesh of the passive woman. As Sadie pushed with a final mighty thrust, the girl cried out in pain, her body tensing then collapsing. She moaned as the candle was pumped into her, fucking her, ripping to shreds the final remnants of maidenhead as blood dribbled down the inside of her leg to the floor of her sacrificial altar. Her hips lurched in response to the pressure of the erect staff inside of her, and despite her pain, or perhaps because of it, she throbbed to orgasm, crying out as her body collapsed.

She lay there, while the sadist tied her hands behind her, and tied down her still-spread legs at the ankles, then stepped down from the altar leaving the candle in her cunt, the flame still twinkling brightly.

I was about to take a shit when the damned Rita sneaked up behind me and cobbed me in the ass. To make matters worse, I had to do it bad, having got the runs from some bad seed the nudists had given me. This sort of thing would never have happened if they fed me hemp, but they didn't, so there I was, screwed in three different ways. Let me tell you, nothing is worse than getting fucked from behind when you have the runs. The pressure comes at you from both ways leaving you with this blob of shit right in the middle of the big intestine. It backs you up like a sewer.

There wasn't much I could do about it once he had mounted, since we were locked in place until he finished. He had been too fast to stop and had gotten on me before I knew what had happened, so I had to wait it out. Rather pissed I was, too. I have a standing principle about not sneaking up on someone you are going to fuck. I believe in Do Unto Others.

Obviously Rita didn't. I shouldn't have been too surprised at that, since it is a sociologically proven fact that homosexual roosters have a certain lack of moral scruples and tend to be unethical. Besides— they gossip. I thought Rita was different, but I had been confusing charm with integrity. Under the circumstances however, I preferred charm. Still, I would make it a point not to turn my back on him again.

After he pulled out, I tried to take a shit, but found myself unable to dislodge the cement-hard mass from my rectum. I figured that I would be constipated for a week.

Up on the altar, the candle was burning closer and closer to the pink shaven flesh of the ex-virgin. In fact, it was getting so close that despite her spread legs, the hot wax dripped on them, dribbling down the insides. The flame had burned down to the slit of her cunt where the rest of the candle was buried. The outside, coated with the frothy milky juices of her aroused and orgasmed cunt, glowed in the candlelight. I thought I noticed something strange and hopped over for a closer look. Sure enough, small bubbles were forming on the wet candle. The flame was boiling the moisture, thick-ening it, turning it into pudding. Cunt pudding!

Mona was screaming. The candle had burned down far enough to boil the pudding. From where I stood I could smell barbecued cunt. A simple sauce brushed over the raw flesh to marinate it, composed of two parts chili sauce, one part red wine, one part avocado peel would have improved the flavor 100%.

But who ever listened to a chicken? Not humans, that's for sure. They think they know everything. Lots of laughs. How many neurotic chickens do they know? How many chickens start forest fires? Do chickens go into politics or beat up hippies? When was the last time *you* got mugged by a chicken?

How many wars are started by chickens?

Humans may scoff at chickens, but we will be around long after they have blown themselves sky high.

The flame finally died, suffocated, no doubt, by the airless wetness inside her cunt. She lay still, eyes closed, breathing as if she were asleep. Sadie climbed up onto the platform and pulled the candle out.

"Throw me the poker!" she yelled at the crowd below. An ebony dildo sailed through the air into her outstretched hand. She kneeled down and separated the lips of the ex-virgin masochist's cunt with her thumb, fore, and middle fingers, stretching the

203

opening wide to accommodate the shaft of wood with which she was about to penetrate Mona's used and burnt flesh.

The prostrate girl groaned as the wood was thrust in, groaning even louder as it was stirred and pumped to and fro, churning and scraping the slick flesh hidden behind the folds of pink that reached out of the opening to shine in the torch light. She arched her back, throwing it against the floor as the ebony carving jammed deeper and more vigorously into her body. Moaning, her stomach muscles were rolling, shoulders beating against the wood below them, bruising black and blue as one dyke after the other took her turn at the base of the dildo, bringing her to orgasm after orgasm, after throbbing burning orgasm. Her armpits, ever wet, literally flooded. After the last dyke had brought her to climax with the great ebony machine, she passed out from exhaustion.

Sadie untied the ropes that bound the girl. Freed, she lay perfectly still as the older woman turned her over. From the fire she pulled a large brand, glowing hot, and placed it sizzling and crackling onto the fatty part of the girl's ass. Mona moaned and scratched at the wooden floor with her nails as the red-hot metal seared deep into her fat. She gasped as it was pulled off.

Consumed by curiosity, I hopped closer to inspect

the mark left by the brand. There, burned forever into the flesh of her ass were the words, BORN TO RAISE HELL.

As she lay on her stomach, still partly unconscious, her legs were still spread wide enough for me to see inside.

What I saw took me back to the dear bygone days of the circus. Memories of the voluptuous Rosie, lying on her back, naked with her legs spread wide to expose her cunt, glistening, large, and inviting, flashed through my mind as I stared at Mona, so similar and yet so different. Waves of nostalgia swept through me as I looked deep into Mona, and the desire to bury myself, to explore, overcame my better judgment.

Slowly, carefully, I approached her and pressed the top of my head into her. She didn't move, so I pressed on further to bury my whole head and part of my shoulders down to my wing tips inside her body. It was wet and airless, just like the Geek's throat, but smelled like fish. It pressed against me, folding me in a sticky cloak that suffocated even my intellect. I floated back to my days in the egg. Its warmth was like the warmth of Mona's body. I was an egg yolk again, and felt young and protected. I wanted to bask forever in it. I closed my eyes and a snatch of music trailed through me.

Suddenly reality gripped me and I knew this

wasn't an egg and that I would suffocate if I didn't get out. I pushed my wing against her pelvis bone and broke away from her body. The feathers of my head and shoulders were covered with sticky, smelly goo. It would be a mammoth clean-up job. As I hopped off the altar I swore never to stick my head in a cunt again. The effects were too scary and it wasn't worth the effort of cleaning my feathers.

Chapter 25

The following morning I hopped silently across the clearing. In a distance I saw the ex-virgin Mona sitting on the altar. I came closer. She was hunched forward, holding to a bottle of Vaseline Petroleum Jelly. She reached into it with her free hand, scooped out a blob and began to smear it over the blistered flesh of her pubic area. Her cunt was in bad shape, red and swollen with large welts. It would peel like hell in a few days. She rubbed slowly, almost caressing the flesh with her fingertips. She reached for yet another blob of Vaseline to mold it thickly on her skin.

I hopped down to the densely wooded area of the island. Soon I reached the spot where the Geek hid most of his wood and string. I noticed with interest the growing pile he had collected. He meant business.

The sound of feet crashing through the underbrush made me turn around quickly. It was the Geek with another armful of branches and vines. He saw me and grunted.

"You. Thought you'd be out cold for the whole day after sticking your head up that pig's cunt. You'd both have gotten what you deserved if you had gotten stuck. She even seemed to like it. Both of you were disgusting."

I clucked, taken aback. The Geek turned from me. He set a small pile of wood under a nearby bush. He hid a smaller pile in a tangle of vines. The last armload he stuck under another bush. Then he sat on a jutting rock and rolled the coarse vines into a ball. This he stashed near the first pile in the bramble bushes. He disappeared into the woods and continued his search. I hopped onward, back to the clearing and amused myself by watching the lady smear Vaseline on her cunt. Her fingers sank deeper into the fleshy recesses of her body to linger, massaging and exploring the newly uncovered passageway.

They spread the opening of her vagina and her

hand, still dripping and covered with Vaseline, thrust deeper and harder, shoving, churning, beating the hungry flesh.

My prick hardened pleasantly, but not urgently. I decided to wait before relieving myself. I hoped I would run into Rita later on.

Chapter 26

That night after dinner, before tying up the Geek, all the campers went over to watch the Indian wrestling match between the Blob Princess and the visitor from the other island. It had been arranged that when one of them had been defeated in the competition, the campers would send up smoke signals to the neighboring nudists, to inform them that they could come and get their man. Every day progress reports had been sent via smoke, to the Gaylord campers. So far there had been no change, since both, staking their pride and reputations on the outcome, refused to give an inch, preferring death in battle to the disgrace of losing.

As the nudists stood in a circle around them, no one spoke a word. No one dared cough or sneeze. The women hardly dared breathe as they watched the two, pale with exhaustion. Both the Blob Princess and the male remained, arms straining upward, and the campers soon became bored.

The Geek went voluntarily to the pole at their signal and waited to be tied. Before they got around to it, he bent down, took me in his hands and waited. They threw the ropes around him, tied the knots and settled comfortably to wait for his act to begin and their desire to be aroused.

Actually I think they were on to me and my act. They must have known from the way I didn't run away that I wasn't afraid and that the fight I put up was nothing but a fake. Still, I had professional pride and my job demanded showmanship. For this reason, when he raised me high above to plunge me into his mouth, I acted afraid, flapped, fought, crowed, and in general gave it all I had. Perhaps someday I would be numbered among the greats of the circus.

After he had finished and acknowledged their applause he set me loose, smiling gloatingly to himself. He knew, as I did, that his time on the island was almost at an end. Progress on the raft was increasing in tempo and he would be ready to set sail in a few days, or as soon as he was able to steal food. This could be a problem since they kept everything but my grain in a special storage bin, but I knew the Geek would find a way.

It was rodeo night, a special brainchild of Roxie's, ever the recreation director.

Spurs, brands, whips, and cowboy hats were passed out to everyone. Those with the sadistic leanings would be cowboys, and the others would be either cattle or horses. Roxie, Sadie, Big Maria, Angelfood and a few of the others donned the glittering spurs and the ten gallon hats, wrapping the whips around their naked waists. A bonfire was built in the middle of the clearing and brands were put on to heat. With their whips, which they used as lassos, they charged Cleo and of course Mona, as well as the others, whooping and whirling the long leather whips above their heads. The masochists were rounded up in the middle of the clearing, surrounded on all sides by the cowgirls. One of the sadists would run into the makeshift pen and tackle one of the steer-women, throwing her to the ground. One of the others would run in, grab a brand and slam it sizzling onto the bare ass of the woman screaming below.

They grabbed Cleo, who began screaming even before they threw her down. As Angelfood galloped at her, arms spread, teeth bared, she gasped and tried to break through the ring of cowgirls who stood in a circle around her and the others. They blocked her escape. Cleo threw her body, slamming against the body of Sadie, trying to knock her down and run over her to freedom. Sadie, whose arms were muscular from so much practice with the whip, cuffed her in the side of the jaw and pushed her backwards, throwing herself on top. She slapped Cleo's face hard with the palm of her hand again, the other cheek with the back, slamming flesh against flesh. Sadie drew her leg up behind her and slammed her knee back down and into Cleo's cunt. The poor would-be escapee screamed, then gasped as Sadie bit the tip of her nose, embedding her front teeth in Cleo's nostrils. Then Sadie rolled off her, stood up and grabbed the prone woman's ankles, dragging her to the center and near the bonfire.

"Gimme a hot one!" she squalled. "This one's a real fighter."

Angelfood pulled a glowing brand from the fire and handed it to the sadist, who slowly lowered it onto and through Cleo's flesh. She screamed as the burning steel was held against her. Sadie pulled it up to leave a steaming red burn in the shape of a small star.

"Gimme another!" yelled the sadist. "She needs to be punished."

"No! No! please!" begged the helpless Cleo. "I don't want to play this any more!"

"You're fulla shit!" rasped Sadie, slurring her speech, for she had been drinking all afternoon.

She grabbed another brand from Angelfood and plunged it down onto the other cheek of Cleo's ass. The woman screamed again, twisting her torso to escape from the cruel metal, and slammed her head against the ground. When Sadie pulled it off, there on the other cheek was a matching, identically placed star, no longer the lone star.

"She's done!" yelled Sadie, as she grabbed Cleo's hair and yanked her to her feet. She whirled her around by it, then kicked her in her branded ass as she stumbled toward the edge of the clearing.

Her progress was blocked by the sadists in spurs and hats and she had to be content to remain inside the clearing at the edge, away from the fire and its glowing brands.

Roxie tackled Mona, throwing her off balance. Instead of sending her to the center to be branded, however, she threw her own body on top of hers. Digging her spurs into Mona's side she waved the whip around her head, yodeling in animal spirits while she sent it crashing down on Mona's ass. Mona, as usual, screamed, loving every minute of it. Roxie yanked the whip over her head again and sent it slamming back down on the tender pink buttocks beneath her. Mona lurched awkwardly forward on her hands and knees, carrying the large woman on her tiny back. Roxie kicked her sides again, piercing the skin once more with the glittering spurs. Blood ran thickly and slowly down Mona's sides, circling under her belly to drip off her navel. Roxie punctured her side once more and other streams of blood oozed out of the holes to mingle with that already dripping off her underbelly. Mona paused to sob violently, her shoulders wrenching from the passion of her feeling and Roxie whipped her again, cutting the leather deep into her skin.

She jumped off and pushed Mona over on her side to her back, spreading her legs harshly apart with both hands. She crawled in between them and planted her mouth over Mona's opening while digging her nails into the girl's thighs. She pushed her head hard against Mona's cunt while her lips on the outside provided an air-tight suction plunger as she drew the liquid from Mona's aroused body into her mouth.

When she had drunk her fill, she pulled her lips away and stood up.

"Why don't you take a douche?" she asked the masochist in a scornful tone.

Mona lay on the ground at her feet looking crushed. Roxie laughed harshly and walked away.

I, for one, was hideously aroused by this. Unfortunately Rita and I were feuding and he would have nothing to do with me. As a result, I was horny. Desperately horny. I hopped over to a tree and tried to rub myself up and down on it. It didn't work and I was as unrelieved as ever. It was throbbing like it had never throbbed before, and the pressure built up inside made it feel as if it were going to blow up. I had to do something and fast before I became unroostered by the tragedy of having my prick blow up in my face.

I hopped on and saw Rita standing in the shadow of an avocado tree. I crowed apologetically at him and waited, head bowed and looking humble. I was desperate. Sure enough, after his pride had been salved, he felt he could come to me and still keep face. I crowed beseechingly and he cackled back. His hen imitation voice had improved while we weren't communicating. Perhaps he had more time to practice. Anyway he came over to me and let me mount him. I plunged deep into him and so relieved my prick of its load. It felt so good.

I happened to look up in time to see the Geek. For some reason, as he watched the ladies in action, he was throwing up all over himself. I couldn't understand this since their most interesting game should have been distracting enough for him to forget any upset from the horrible food they were feeding him.

Roxie went over to him and untied his knots. He promptly walked away from the clearing in the direction of his hut.

After the pole had been freed from its occupant, Sadie and Roxie grabbed Mona and slammed her back-first against it, tying her legs, arms and body to it with a stout rope, leaving one arm free. She stood wide-eyed in fearfully joyful anticipation. She bit her lips as sweat rolled out of her pores and down her body. While the two women were seeing that she was securely tied, Angelfood placed a little metal holder of long pearl-tipped hatpins into the fire, taking care to keep the tips away from the flame and from melting.

After the hatpins had been in there a while, Angelfood pulled one out by the still-cool top, gingerly carrying it over to the bound Mona. As the girl stood, bound and fearful, the negress slowly and deliberately pressed it against the flesh of the girl's left breast, pressing it until it broke the skin, until it was buried deep in Mona's mammary. The girl screamed, groaned and sobbed, pleading for mercy. Angelfood laughed seductively in her rich, mellow, contralto tones.

Sweat ran down Mona's face and the whites of her eyes glowed as she lifted her head and rolled them toward the sky above. She whimpered as Sadie slithered toward her, the pin raised like a stiletto, to plunge it through the tip of her raised and hardened nipple into the tissues and glands of her breast. Mona groaned in tortured agony and begged for death to release her, while her free hand pressed against the opening of her cunt, to squeeze and bring relief to the throbbing folds of flesh hidden just above the soft flaps of skin between her legs. After pumping, while yet another pin was plunged into her breast, she pulled the fingers, now coated with wetness, out of her. She rolled her head from side to side, her face contorted in dismay.

Rita sneaked up from behind and thrust his cock into me again like he did the other night. Fortunately I didn't have to take a shit so I didn't mind it as much. Actually, I rather enjoyed it and decided to let the hemorrhoids be hanged. It felt quite good, actually, better than it felt before. Perhaps it was just a case of getting stretched enough to handle it. It had an added advantage in that it didn't block my view, so I could watch as Sadie and Roxie and Big Maria gathered wood and piled it at Mona's feet. Then they went to the trash barrel and pulled out old newspapers. Crumpling them, they then piled the old newspapers at her feet as well.

"We are going to give you, little one, the greatest thrill any masochist could ever wish for."

"Not to mention a gigantic orgasm the likes of which you could never have again!"

"And you will provide wonderful entertainment for the whole camp!" said Roxie the Recreation Director as she struck a match.

A glaze passed over Mona's eyes and a blank smile spread across her face. She breathed heavily. Her body writhed under the ropes and her hips began to undulate as best they could despite being tied up. She ran her tongue across her front teeth as Roxie bent down and set the papers on fire. Sadie poured some gasoline on the flames and they leaped high around Mona's helpless body. She screamed, writhing as she began to laugh wildly. She moaned as her hand went down once more and thrust deep into her cunt. As the flames surrounded her, growing higher as they consumed her body, she was seen, her fingers pumping the plump sensitive flesh of the passage to her womb. She moaned, smiling and licking her parched lips as she rolled her eyes heavenward, the flames crackling around her. The sizzling grew louder as the smell of burning flesh filled the air.

Rita's weight pressed down on my back as his prick surged its load out into my anus. I could feel the throbbing from behind as the liquid gushed out in spurts. His body shuddered on top of me as he released the last of his semen in me and I crowed at the force.

I noticed, out of the corner of my eye, as I was

catching my breath, that the Geek was taking advantage of the distraction of Mona being burned alive to break into the food supply. He stole away, taking the long way around the clearing and through the woods, with loaves of bread tucked under one arm and beef jerky under the other. In his hands he clutched two jugs of bottled water.

I decided I had better keep my eye on the Geek so that I could escape when he did. After Rita pulled out of me, I hopped off to follow the Geek wherever he was going.

Chapter 27

By the following morning the Geek had nearly
finished the raft. It was an ugly thing, made out of
bits and pieces of random wood. Lashed together
with the vine that grew wild on the island, it looked
as if it would fall apart with the first wave. I had
second thoughts about leaving with him, since I
could think of better ways to die than to drown
somewhere in the middle of the Pacific. It seemed
so inappropriate somehow. On the raft, made of
bamboo and woven together palm fronds, was a
tiny shelter, large enough to hold the supplies and

provide a place for the Geek and me to sleep. He grunted when he saw me and continued to put the finishing touches on the raft.

As the tide started to go out, he dragged his creation to the water and waded beside it as he pulled it in. I jumped on before he got it all the way past the sand and took shelter in the little hut. Stored neatly inside was the food and water as well as the woolen blanket he had stolen from his hut.

Finally we floated out past the breakers, lurching on rough choppy waters for the rest of the day. Night fell and the ocean, although choppy, was peaceful. Toward night of the following day we washed upon a deserted beach.

We wandered along the rocky coast taking shelter for the night under a huge boulder. It was cold and all we had was the woolen blanket for warmth.

As soon as daybreak made it light enough to see, we got up and continued to search for civilization. As the Geek walked, blanket wrapped around his hips, I perched on his shoulder. We climbed over the rocks and boulders of the rough terrain.

Up ahead we saw a gatelike entrance coming out of a cave under the mountain we were about to climb.

The Geek climbed up the pile of rocks that blocked the path to the old wood and stone entrance. When he finally reached it, huffing and panting, he clenched the rope that hung from the blackened silver bell. It pealed out treble vibrations as the Geek waited hopefully. We heard the soft padding of feet as the door was unbolted and pushed open, creaking. In it stood a man about sixty-five, fat and bald, wearing a gray homespun robe tied at the waist. He bowed his head, then raised it to address the Geek.

"May I be of some service to you, brother?" he asked quietly.

"I don't know," said the Geek. "You see, my chicken and I just escaped from where we were being held prisoner on this island by some bulldyke nudists. We've been floating for about two days on this raft I strung together out of old branches and things. We don't have any more food and last night we had to sleep under a rock."

The old man first looked amazed, then sympathetic.

"You've had a very trying time, haven't you brother? I think we can help you here."

"Even if you could feed us and give us a dry warm place for the night..." said the Geek, his lip quivering.

"Of course. You are welcome to stay with us as long as you wish."

"Who are you?" asked the Geek. "And what is this place?"

"My name is Father Pepito. You are in a monastery of the order of Discordia, a rare sect of central African Christians. Because of its outrageous interpretation of the scriptures it has been condemned by all the world's faiths, including probably your own."

"I am an anarchist."

"You follow the gospel of anarchy? Perhaps you are more compatible with our teachings than I thought. The rest of the faiths would burn us at the stake for heresy."

"But people don't burn other people at the stake any more," said the Geek in amazement.

"Not even in Spain?" asked the monk, looking amazed.

"They stopped doing that about three hundred years ago. Where have you been all your life?" asked the Geek, wide-eyed.

"Here," said the fat robed man.

"You must have had a childhood, a life somewhere else before you became a monk."

"No, I've lived here since birth."

"You were born here, in the monastery I suppose?" said the Geek in a tone of thinly disguised sarcasm.

"That's right. Because we have to remain hidden if we are to survive we breed our own followers. The holy fathers and the holy mothers in the adjoining convent get together when the moon is full and

226

produce babies, which are then in nine months delivered by the holy midwife. The girl babies are taken by the nuns and the monks raise the boys."

"How cozy."

"True, but it has its disadvantages. We have been cut off from civilization for three hundred years, since the time we first came to this wilderness."

"You mean America."

"If that's what they call it," said the monk as he motioned for us to follow him. He led us down the winding mazelike corridors of the underground retreat, far into the bowels of Mother Earth. The passage widened and up ahead we saw a large room leading back into other large rooms and seating about ten monks, all dressed like Father Pepito. As the Geek and I passed through them they smiled at us in welcome.

The Geek began crying openly.

"What is the matter, brother?" asked Father Pepito.

"It's all so beautiful!" sobbed the Geek. "After what I've been through, this peaceful monastery is heaven."

"Would you like to stay here forever, join us and become one of us?" asked the little monk.

A radiant smile spread across the Geek's face as he looked around at the benign faces of the men.

"Oh yes. They all look so happy."

"We'll confirm you at communion this afternoon!"

"Communion? Does that mean wine? I can't handle the stuff. Never could."

"Nonsense. This is communion wine. It is sanctified, and is something you *must* drink in order to become one of us."

"Well, all right, but I've never been able to drink wine. Even the smallest amount gets me sick and totally drunk. It's something in my body."

"I doubt if you'll have the same trouble with *this*. It is some of the very wine Our Savior turned *into* water. You only get it once in your whole life, when you are confirmed as a Discordian monk. And you are given only a small amount."

"That's fascinating!" said the Geek. "How did you get this wine?"

"The founder of our faith stole it from the wedding where the miracle took place. Because he did, and we now have the fruit of his thievery, we know and can prove that we have the True Faith. The others persecute us out of jealousy."

"That is so touching!" exclaimed the Geek, sobbing anew.

"Yes. Now I will take you to your cell… You must pray until we come and take you to the chapel."

Father Pepito led the Geek away, but I decided

not to go with him. Instead I explored the maze of caves that hid the monastery.

After I had investigated about five rooms, I smelled grain. Hemp! I crowed in anticipation as I hopped, flapping toward the source of the fragrance.

Off to one side, in a small dead end room was not only a huge sack of it, but also, roosting on top, a hen more beautiful, glowing and fluffy than even Hilda. She clucked coyly at me, rolling her shiny black eyes. I crowed exultantly, beating my wings as I approached to mount her.

From behind I heard another crowing. I whirled around, angry with the intruder. There stood a rooster, black eyes burning, comb red and quivering with rage. He headed toward me. I crowed at him, incensed. He jumped me and tore at my lovely pink comb. I crowed in pain and tried to throw him from me. He held on, digging his claws through my feathers and into my flesh. I felt their points puncture my skin and the blood welling out of the holes. I crowed again, twisting my neck to jab him in the side with my beak. I got him and he crowed in pain but didn't let go. I flapped suddenly backward and threw him off balance. I attacked, charging at him with my wings flapping and my beak poised for the kill. He jumped out of the way and leaped onto me again. He tore into my wing, ripping the feathers

out and gouging the flesh. He rammed it into the
back of my neck as I tried to twist again and unbal-
ance him. By doubling up and rolling, I managed to
unseat him again. By now the hen looked less and
less attractive, so I decided to get out while I was
still alive. I headed back in the direction of the
Geek. Part way there, I saw the monks lead him to
the chapel. I followed.

They placed him kneeling before the altar. Two
candles were lit and incense was burned. Then
Father Pepito stood before him and lowered the
small glass of wine to the Geek's lips, and after he
had drunk it, put it back on the altar.

He motioned for the Geek to stand. He stood,
teetering to his feet, catching his balance on the
railing that separated him from the altar. One of
the monks grabbed his arm to help him keep his
balance.

"I...I think I'm going to throw up," said the
Geek. "Wine always does this to me. I'm sorry."

"That's all right; regrettable, but forgivable. I'll
show you to the monastery potty."

"You have toilets?" the Geek asked in amazement. "I thought you had been out of touch with
civilization for three hundred years."

"You've been talking to Pops Pepito. He's a little
weird in his old age. We do keep isolated but it's not
as bad as all that. We younger ones go into town all

the time. We get stared at because of our robes, but we have no trouble otherwise."

"Then you aren't persecuted?"

"Not really. It stopped about the time they stopped bothering witches. Father Pepito lives in the past."

"How sad for him."

"Not really. He's happy. It's true we're not well known and prefer to keep it that way. For that reason we don't mingle as much as we could, but when a good thing like indoor plumbing comes along, we have it installed. It was rather difficult having it put in the cave, not to mention expensive, but we did it anyway. We young ones believe in progress, even if the Father Pepitos of our order don't."

"Well, what do you do for money to pay for things like indoor plumbing and trips to town?" asked the Geek.

"Grow marijuana and sell it through our distributor."

"Free enterprise is alive and well," said the Geek.

As I followed, the young monk led him into a small room near to the hemp seed and hen room. He stood at the door as the Geek staggered in.

"Will you be all right or do you want me to stay with you?"

"I'll be all right," said the Geek, bending over the toilet.

He kneeled in front of the porcelain bowl as the monk walked away. He gagged, pushing the muscles below his chin down and his mouth open. His chest heaved and the half-digested contents of his stomach splattered out into the toilet. He stood up, bent over and threw up once more. As he collapsed over the bowl he hit his head on the rim while his legs dangled onto the floor. I heard a strange bubbling sound echoing out from within the bowl. The body of the Geek, half hanging from the seat, remained still. I waited. No movement. The bubbling had stopped and still not a muscle in his body even twitched.

Poor Geek.

Chapter 28

I decided there was nothing here for me. I felt yearning for my old circus days. The siren call of the calliope floated through my brain, boiling my blood with thoughts of adventure and glory.

I hopped through the maze-like passageway to the gate. It was closed, but I climbed a bush that was growing inside and made it over the top.

I climbed down the path and around in a direction where my instincts told me there might be a circus. I flapped as fast as my wings would carry me, as I remembered the smell of popcorn and cotton candy.

Somewhere out there was another geek. A Geek without a chicken. I would find that geek and make him *my* Geek.

On I traveled, never wearying.

A chicken in search of a Geek.

The Masquerade Erotic Newsletter

> *"Here's a very provocative, very professional [newsletter]...made up of intelligent erotic writing... Stimulating, yet not sleazy photos add to the picture and also help make this zine a high quality publication."* —Gray Areas

From **Masquerade Books**, the World's Leading Publisher of Erotica, comes *The Masquerade Erotic Newsletter*—the best source for provocative, cutting-edge fiction, sizzling pictorials, scintillating and illuminating exposes of the sex industry, and probing reviews of the latest books and videos.

Featured writers and articles have included:

Lars Eighner • *Why I Write Gay Erotica*
Pat Califia • *Among Us, Against Us*
Felice Picano • *An Interview with Samuel R. Delany*
Samuel R. Delany • *The Mad Man* (excerpt)
Maxim Jakubowski • *Essex House: The Rise and Fall of Speculative Erotica*
Red Jordan Arobateau • *Reflections of a Lesbian Trick*
Aaron Travis • *Lust*
Nancy Ava Miller, M. Ed. • *Beyond Personal*
Tuppy Owens • *Female Erotica in Great Britain*
Trish Thomas • *From Dyke to Dude*
Barbara Nitke • *Resurrection*
and many more....

The newsletter has also featured stunning photo essays by such masters of fetish photography as **Robert Chouraqui**, **Eric Kroll**, **Richard Kern**, and **Trevor Watson**.

A one-year subscription (6 issues) to the *Newsletter* costs $30.00. Use the accompanying coupon to subscribe now—for an uninterrupted string of the most provocative of pleasures (as well as a special gift, offered to subscribers only!).

Free
GIFT

ROSEBUD BOOKS

THE ROSEBUD READER

Rosebud Books—the hottest-selling line of lesbian erotica available—here collects the very best of the best. Rosebud has contributed greatly to the burgeoning genre of lesbian erotica—to the point that authors like Lindsay Welsh, Aarona Griffin and Valentina Cilescu are among the hottest and most closely watched names in lesbian and gay publishing. Here are the finest moments from Rosebud's contemporary classics. $5.95/319-8

LOVECHILD
GAG

From New York's thriving poetry scene comes this explosive volume of work from one of the bravest, most cutting young writers you'll ever encounter. The poems in *Gag* take on American hypocrisy with uncommon insight and energy, and announce Lovechild as a writer of unique and unforgettable rage.
$5.95/369-4

ALISON TYLER
THE BLUE ROSE

The tale of a modern sorority—fashioned after a Victorian girls' school. Ignited to the heights of passion by erotic tales of the Victorian age, a group of lusty young women are encouraged to act out their forbidden fantasies—all under the tutelage of Mistresses Emily and Justine, two avid practitioners of hard-core discipline! $5.95/335-X

ELIZABETH OLIVER
PAGAN DREAMS

Cassidy and Samantha plan a vacation at a secluded bed-and-breakfast, hoping for a little personal time alone. Their hostess, however, has different plans. The lovers are plunged into a world of dungeons and pagan rites, as the merciless Anastasia steals Samantha for her own. B&B—B&D-style! $5.95/295-7

SUSAN ANDERS
PINK CHAMPAGNE

Tasty, torrid tales of butch/femme couplings—from a writer more than capable of describing the special fire ignited when opposites collide. Tough as nails or soft as silk, these women seek out their antitheses, intent on working out the details of their own personal theory of difference. $5.95/282-5

LAVENDER ROSE
Anonymous

A classic collection of lesbian literature: From the writings of Sappho, Queen of the island Lesbos, to the turn-of-the-century *Black Book of Lesbianism*; from *Tips to Maidens* to *Crimson Hairs*, a recent lesbian saga—here are the great but little-known lesbian writings and revelations. $4.95/208-6

EDITED BY LAURA ANTONIOU
LEATHERWOMEN II

A follow-up volume to the popular and controversial *Leatherwomen*. Laura Antoniou turns an editor's discerning eye to the writing of women on the edge—resulting in a collection sure to ignite libidinal flames. Leave taboos behind—because these Leatherwomen know no limits.... $4.95/229-9

LEATHERWOMEN

These fantasies, from the pens of new or emerging authors, break every rule imposed on women's fantasies. The hottest stories from some of today's newest and most outrageous writers make this an unforgettable exploration of the female libido. $4.95/3095-4

ROSEBUD BOOKS

LESLIE CAMERON

THE WHISPER OF FANS

"Just looking into her eyes, she felt that she knew a lot about this woman. She could see strength, boldness, a fresh sense of aliveness that rocked her to the core. In turn she felt open, revealed under the woman's gaze—all her secrets already told. No need of shame or artifice...." $5.95/259-0

AARONA GRIFFIN

PASSAGE AND OTHER STORIES

An S/M romance. Lovely Nina is frightened by her lesbian passions until she finds herself infatuated with a woman she spots at a local café. One night Nina follows her and finds herself enmeshed in an endless maze leading to a world where women test the edges of sexuality and power. $4.95/3057-1

VALENTINA CILESCU

THE ROSEBUD SUTRA

"Women are hardly ever known in their true light, though they may love others, or become indifferent towards them, may give them delight, or abandon them, or may extract from them all the wealth that they possess." So says *The Rosebud Sutra*—a volume promising women's inner secrets. One woman learns to use these secrets in a quest for pleasure with a succession of lady loves.... $4.95/242-6

THE HAVEN

The shocking story of a dangerous woman on the run—and the innocents she takes with her on a trip to Hell. J craves domination, and her perverse appetites lead her to the Haven: the isolated sanctuary Ros and Annie call home. Soon J forces her way into the couple's world, bringing unspeakable lust and cruelty into their lives. The Dominatrix Who Came to Dinner! $4.95/165-9

MISTRESS MINE

Sophia Cranleigh sits in prison, accused of authoring the "obscene" *Mistress Mine*. For Sophia has led no ordinary life, but has slaved and suffered—deliciously—under the hand of the notorious Mistress Malin. How long had she languished under the dominance of this incredible beauty? $4.95/109-8

LINDSAY WELSH

THE BEST OF LINDSAY WELSH

A collection of this popular writer's best work. This author was one of Rosebud's early bestsellers, and remains highly popular. A sampler set to introduce some of the hottest lesbian erotica to a wider audience. $5.95/368-6

PROVINCETOWN SUMMER

This completely original collection is devoted exclusively to white-hot desire between women. From the casual encounters of women on the prowl to the enduring erotic bonds between old lovers, the women of *Provincetown Summer* will set your senses on fire! A national best-seller. $5.95/362-7

NECESSARY EVIL

What's a girl to do? When her Mistress proves too systematic, too by-the-book, one lovely submissive takes the ultimate chance—choosing and creating a Mistress who'll fulfill her heart's desire. Little did she know how difficult it would be—and, in the end, rewarding.... $5.95/277-9

A VICTORIAN ROMANCE

Lust-letters from the road. A young Englishwoman realizes her dream—a trip abroad under the guidance of her eccentric maiden aunt. Soon the young but blossoming Elaine comes to discover her own sexual talents, as a hot-blooded Parisian named Madelaine takes her Sapphic education in hand. $5.95/365-1

ROSEBUD BOOKS

A CIRCLE OF FRIENDS
The author of the nationally best-selling *Provincetown Summer* returns with the story of a remarkable group of women. Slowly, the women pair off to explore all the possibilities of lesbian passion, until finally it seems that there is nothing—and no one—they have not dabbled in. A stunning tribute to truly special relationships. $4.95/250-7

PRIVATE LESSONS
A high voltage tale of life at The Whitfield Academy for Young Women—where cruel headmistress Devon Whitfield presides over the in-depth education of only the most talented and delicious of maidens. Elizabeth Dunn arrives at the Academy, where it becomes clear that she has much to learn—to the delight of Devon Whitfield and her randy staff of Mistresses! Another contemporary classic from Lindsay Welsh. $4.95/116-0

BAD HABITS
What does one do with a poorly trained slave? Break her of her bad habits, of course! The story of te ultimate finishing school, *Bad Habits* was an immediate favorite with women nationwide. "Talk about passing the wet test!... If you like hot, lesbian erotica, run—don't walk...and pick up a copy of *Bad Habits*."—*Lambda Book Report* $4.95/3068-7

ANNABELLE BARKER

MOROCCO
A luscious young woman stands to inherit a fortune—if she can only withstand the ministrations of her cruel guardian until her twentieth birthday. With two months left, Lila makes a bold bid for freedom, only to find that liberty has its own excruciating and delicious price.... $4.95/148-9

A.L. REINE

DISTANT LOVE & OTHER STORIES
A book of seductive tales. In the title story, Leah Michaels and her lover Ranelle have had four years of blissful, smoldering passion together. One night, when Ranelle is out of town, Leah records an audio "Valentine," a cassette filled with erotic reminiscences.... $4.95/3056-3

RHINOCEROS BOOKS

EDITED BY AMARANTHA KNIGHT

FLESH FANTASTIC
Humans have long toyed with the idea of "playing God": creating life from nothingness, bringing Life to the inanimate. Now Amarantha Knight, author of the "Darker Passions" series of erotic horror novels, collects stories exploring not only the allure of Creation, but the lust that follows.... One of our most shocking and sexy anthologies. $6.95/352-X

GARY BOWEN

DIARY OF A VAMPIRE
"Gifted with a darkly sensual vision and a fresh voice, [Bowen] is a writer to watch out for." —Cecilia Tan
The chilling, arousing, and ultimately moving memoirs of an undead—but all too human—soul. Bowen's Rafael, a red-blooded male with an insatiable hunger for same, is the perfect antidote to the effete malcontents haunting bookstores today. *Diary of a Vampire* marks the emergence of a bold and brilliant vision, firmly rooted in past *and* present. $6.95/331-7

RHINOCEROS BOOKS

RENÉ MAIZEROY

FLESHLY ATTRACTIONS

Lucien Hardanges was the son of the wantonly beautiful actress, Marie-Rose Hardanges. When she decides to let a "friend" introduce her son to the pleasures of love, Marie-Rose could not have foretold the erotic excesses that would lead to her own ruin and that of her cherished son. $6.95/299-X

EDITED BY LAURA ANTONIOU

NO OTHER TRIBUTE

A collection of stories sure to challenge Political Correctness in a way few have before, with tales of women kept in bondage to their lovers by their deepest passions. Love pushes these women beyond acceptable limits, rendering them helpless to deny the men and women they adore. A companion volume to *By Her Subdued*. $6.95/294-9

SOME WOMEN

Over forty essays written by women actively involved in consensual dominance and submission. Professional mistresses, lifestyle leatherdykes, whipmakers, titleholders—women from every conceivable walk of life lay bare their true feelings about about issues as explosive as feminism, abuse, pleasures and public image. $6.95/300-7

BY HER SUBDUED

Stories of women who get what they want. The tales in this collection all involve women in control—of their lives, their loves, their men. So much in control, in fact, that they can remorselessly break rules to become the powerful goddesses of the men who sacrifice all to worship at their feet. $6.95/281-7

JEAN STINE

SEASON OF THE WITCH

"A future in which it is technically possible to transfer the total mind... of a rapist killer into the brain dead but physically living body of his female victim. Remarkable for intense psychological technique. There is eroticism but it is necessary to mark the differences between the sexes and the subtle altering of a man into a woman." —*The Science Fiction Critic* $6.95/268-X

JOHN WARREN

THE TORQUEMADA KILLER

Detective Eva Hernandez has finally gotten her first "big case": a string of vicious murders taking place within New York's SM community. Piece by piece, Eva assembles the evidence, revealing a picture of a world misunderstood and under attack—and gradually comes to understand her own place within it. A hot, edge-of-the-seat thriller from the author of *The Loving Dominant*—and an exciting insider's perspective on "the scene." $6.95/367-8

THE LOVING DOMINANT

Everything you need to know about an infamous sexual variation—and an unspoken type of love. Mentor—a longtime player in the dominance/submission scene—guides readers through this world and reveals the too-often hidden basis of the D/S relationship: care, trust and love. $6.95/218-3

GRANT ANTREWS

SUBMISSIONS

Once again, Antrews portrays the very special elements of the dominant/submissive relationship...with restraint—this time with the story of a lonely man, a winning lottery ticket, and a demanding dominatrix. One of erotica's most discerning writers. $6.95/207-8

RHINOCEROS BOOKS

MY DARLING DOMINATRIX

When a man and a woman fall in love it's supposed to be simple, uncompli-
cated, easy—unless that woman happens to be a dominatrix. Curiosity gives
way to unblushing desire in this story of one man's awakening to the joys to
be experienced as the willing slave of a powerful woman. $6.95/3055-5

LAURA ANTONIOU WRITING AS "SARA ADAMSON"

THE TRAINER

The long-awaited conclusion of Adamson's stunning Marketplace Trilogy!
The ultimate underground sexual realm includes not only willing slaves, but
the exquisite trainers who take submissives firmly in hand. And it is now the
time for these mentors to divulge their own secrets—the desires that led
them to become the ultimate figures of authority. $6.95/249-3

THE SLAVE

The second volume in the "Marketplace" trilogy. *The Slave* covers the experience of one exceptionally talented submissive who longs to join the ranks of
those who have proven themselves worthy of entry into the Marketplace. But
the price, while delicious, is staggeringly high.... Adamson's plot thickens, as
her trilogy moves to a conclusion in *The Trainer*. $6.95/173-X

THE MARKETPLACE

"Merchandise does not come easily to the Marketplace.... They haunt the
clubs and the organizations.... Some of them are so ripe that they intimidate
the poseurs, the weekend sadists and the furtive dilettantes who are so
endemic to that world. And they never stop asking where we may be
found...." $6.95/3096-2

THE CATALYST

After viewing a controversial, explicitly kinky film full of images of bondage and
submission, several audience members find themselves deeply moved by the erotic
suggestions they've seen on the screen. "Sara Adamson"'s sensational debut
volume! $5.95/328-7

DAVID AARON CLARK

SISTER RADIANCE

A chronicle of obsession, rife with Clark's trademark vivisections of contemporary desires, sacred and profane. The vicissitudes of lust and romance are
examined against a backdrop of urban decay and shallow fashionability in this
testament to the allure—and inevitability—of the forbidden. $6.95/215-9

THE WET FOREVER

The story of Janus and Madchen, a small-time hood and a beautiful sex work-
er, *The Wet Forever* examines themes of loyalty, sacrifice, redemption and
obsession amidst Manhattan's sex parlors and underground S/M clubs. Its
combination of sex and suspense led Terence Sellers to proclaim it "evoca-
tive and poetic." $6.95/117-9

ALICE JOANOU

BLACK TONGUE

**"Joanou has created a series of sumptuous, brooding, dark visions of sexu-
al obsession and is undoubtedly a name to look out for in the future."**
                                                              —*Redeemer*

Another seductive book of dreams from the author of the acclaimed
Tourniquet. Exploring lust at its most florid and unsparing, *Black Tongue* is a
trove of baroque fantasies—each redolent of the forbidden. Joanou creates
some of erotica's most mesmerizing and unforgettable characters. $6.95/258-2

TOURNIQUET

A heady collection of stories and effusions from the pen of one our most dazzling young writers. Strange tales abound, from the story of the mysterious and cruel Cybele, to an encounter with the sadistic entertainment of a bizarre after-hours cafe. A sumptuous feast for all the senses..　　$6.95/3060-1

CANNIBAL FLOWER

"She is waiting in her darkened bedroom, as she has waited throughout history, to seduce the men who are foolish enough to be blinded by her irresistible charms....She is the goddess of sexuality, and *Cannibal Flower* is her haunting siren song."—Michael Perkins　　$4.95/72-6

MICHAEL PERKINS

EVIL COMPANIONS

Set in New York City during the tumultuous waning years of the Sixties, *Evil Companions* has been hailed as "a frightening classic." A young couple explores the nether reaches of the erotic unconscious in a shocking confrontation with the extremes of passion. With a new introduction by science fiction legend Samuel R. Delany.　　$6.95/3067-9

AN ANTHOLOGY OF CLASSIC ANONYMOUS EROTIC WRITING

Michael Perkins, acclaimed authority on erotic literature, has collected the very best passages from the world's erotic writing—especially for Rhino*ceros* readers. "Anonymous" is one of the most infamous bylines in publishing history—and these steamy excerpts show why!　　$6.95/140-3

THE SECRET RECORD: Modern Erotic Literature

Michael Perkins, a renowned author and critic of sexually explicit fiction, surveys the field with authority and unique insight. Updated and revised to include the latest trends, tastes, and developments in this misunderstood and maligned genre. An important volume for every erotic reader and fan of high quality adult fiction.　　$6.95/3039-3

HELEN HENLEY

ENTER WITH TRUMPETS

Helen Henley was told that woman just don't write about sex—much less the taboos she was so interested in exploring. So Henley did it alone, flying in the face of "tradition" by producing *Enter With Trumpets*, a touching tale of arousal and devotion in one couple's kinky relationship.　　$6.95/197-7

PHILIP JOSE FARMER

FLESH

Space Commander Stagg explored the galaxies for 800 years, and could only hope that he would be welcomed home by an adoring—or at least *appreciative*—public. Upon his return, the hero Stagg is made the centerpiece of an incredible public ritual—one that will repeatedly take him to the heights of ecstasy, and inexorably drag him toward the depths of hell.　　$6.95/303-1

A FEAST UNKNOWN

"Sprawling, brawling, shocking, suspenseful, hilarious..."

—Theodore Sturgeon

Farmer's supreme anti-hero returns. *A Feast Unknown* begins in 1968, with Lord Grandrith's stunning statement: "I was conceived and born in 1888." Slowly, Lord Grandrith—armed with the belief that he is the son of Jack the Ripper—tells the story of his remarkable and unbridled life. Beginning with his discovery of the secret of immortality, Grandrith's tale proves him no raving lunatic—but something far more bizarre....　　$6.95/276-0

RHINOCEROS BOOKS

THE IMAGE OF THE BEAST

Herald Childe has seen Hell, glimpsed its horror in an act of sexual mutilation. Childe must now find and destroy an inhuman predator through the streets of a polluted and decadent Los Angeles of the future. One clue after another leads Childe to an inescapable realization about the nature of sex and evil.... $6.95/166-7

SAMUEL R. DELANY

EQUINOX

The *Scorpion* has sailed the seas in a quest for every possible pleasure. Her crew is a collection of the young, the twisted, the insatiable. A drifter comes into their midst, and is taken on a fantastic journey to the darkest, most dangerous sexual extremes—until he is finally a victim to their boundless appetites. Delany's classic *The Tides of Lust*, now issued under the author's original title. $6.95/157-8

ANDREI CODRESCU

THE REPENTANCE OF LORRAINE

"One of our most prodigiously talented and magical writers."
—*NYT Book Review*

An aspiring writer, a professor's wife, a secretary, gold anklets, Maoists, Roman harlots—and more—swirl through this spicy tale of a harried quest for a mythic artifact. Written when the author was a young man, this lusty yarn was inspired by the heady days of the Sixties. Includes a new Introduction by the author, painting a portrait of *Lorraine*'s creation. $6.95/329-5

DAVID MELTZER

ORF

He is the ultimate musician-hero—the idol of thousands, the fevered dream of many more. And like many musicians before him, he is misunderstood, misused—and totally out of control. Every last drop of feeling is squeezed from a modern-day troubadour and his lady love. $6.95/110-1

LEOPOLD VON SACHER-MASOCH

VENUS IN FURS

This classic 19th century novel is the first uncompromising exploration of the dominant/submissive relationship in literature. The alliance of Severin and Wanda epitomizes Sacher-Masoch's dark obsession with a cruel, controlling goddess and the urges that drive the man held in her thrall. Includes the letters exchanged between Sacher-Masoch and Emilie Mataja—an aspiring writer he sought as the avatar of his forbidden desires. $6.95/3089-X

SOPHIE GALLEYMORE BIRD

MANEATER

Through a bizarre act of creation, a man attains the "perfect" lover—by all appearances a beautiful, sensuous woman but in reality something far darker. Once brought to life she will accept no mate, seeking instead the prey that will sate her hunger for vengeance. A biting take on the war of the sexes, this debut goes for the jugular of the "perfect woman" myth. $6.95/103-9

TUPPY OWENS

SENSATIONS

A piece of porn history. Tuppy Owens tells the unexpurgated story of the making of *Sensations*—the first big-budget sex flick. Originally commissioned to appear in book form after the release of the film in 1975, *Sensations* is finally released under Masquerade's stylish Rhinoceros imprint. $6.95/3081-4

RHINOCEROS BOOKS

DANIEL VIAN

ILLUSIONS

Two disturbing tales of danger and desire in Berlin on the eve of WWII. From private homes to lurid cafés to decaying streets, passion is explored, exposed, and placed in stark contrast to the brutal violence of the time. A singularly arousing volume. $6.95/3074-1

PERSUASIONS

"The stockings are drawn tight by the suspender belt, tight enough to be stretched to the limit just above the middle part of her thighs..." A double novel, including the classics *Adagio* and *Gabriela and the General*, this volume traces desire around the globe. International lust! $6.95/183-7

LIESEL KULIG

LOVE IN WARTIME

An uncompromising look at the politics, perils and pleasures of sexual power. Madeleine knew that the handsome SS officer was a dangerous man. But she was just a cabaret singer in Nazi-occupied Paris, trying to survive in a perilous time. When Josef fell in love with her, he discovered that a beautiful and amoral woman can sometimes be wildly dangerous. $6.95/3044-X

MASQUERADE BOOKS

LA DOMME: A DOMINATRIX ANTHOLOGY   *Edited by Claire Baeder*
A steamy smorgasbord of female domination! Erotic literature has long been filled with heartstopping portraits of domineering women, and now the most memorable come together in one beautifully brutal volume. No fan of real woman power can afford to miss this ultimate compendium. $5.95/366-X

THE GEEK   *Tiny Alice*
"An adventure novel told by a sex-bent male mini-pygmy. This is an accomplishment of which anybody may be proud."

—Philip José Farmer

A notorious cult classic. *The Geek* is told from the point of view of, well, a chicken who reports on the various perversities he witnesses as part of a traveling carnival. When a gang of renegade lesbians kidnaps Chicken and his geek, all hell breaks loose. A strange tale, filled with outrageous erotic oddities, that finally returns to print after years of infamy. $5.95/341-4

SEX ON THE NET   *Charisse van der Lyn*
Electrifying erotica from one of the Internet's hottest and most widely read authors. Encounters of all kinds—straight, lesbian, dominant/submissive and all sorts of extreme passions—are explored in thrilling detail. Discover what's turning on hackers from coast to coast! $5.95/399-6

BEAUTY OF THE BEAST   *Carole Remy*
A shocking tell-all, written from the point-of-view of a prize-winning reporter. And what reporting she does! All the secrets of an uninhibited life are revealed, and each lusty tableau is painted in glowing colors. Join in on her scandalous adventures—and reap the rewards of her extensive background in Erotic Affairs! $5.95/332-5

NAUGHTY MESSAGE   *Stanley Carten*
Wesley Arthur, a withdrawn computer engineer, discovers a lascivious message on his answering machine. Aroused beyond his wildest dreams by the unmentionable acts described, Wesley becomes obsessed with tracking down the woman behind the seductive voice. His search takes him through strip clubs and no-tell motels—and finally to his randy reward.... $5.95/333-3

MASQUERADE BOOKS

The Marquis de Sade's JULIETTE   *David Aaron Clark*

The Marquis de Sade's infamous Juliette returns—and at the hand of David Aaron Clark, she emerges as the most powerful, perverse and destructive nightstalker modern New York will ever know. Under this domina's tutelage, two women come to know torture's bizarre attractions, as they grapple with the price of Juliette's promise of immortality.

Praise for Dave Clark:

"David Aaron Clark has delved into one of the most sensationalistically taboo aspects of eros, sadomasochism, and produced a novel of unmistakable literary imagination and artistic value."   —Carlo McCormick, *Paper*

$5.95/240-X

THE PARLOR   *N.T. Morley*

Lovely Kathryn gives in to the ultimate temptation. The mysterious John and Sarah ask her to be their slave—an idea that turns Kathryn on so much that she can't refuse! But who are these two mysterious strangers? Little by little, Kathryn comes to know the inner secrets of her stunning keepers. Soon, all is revealed—to the delight of everyone involved! $5.95/291-4

NADIA   *Anonymous*

"Nadia married General the Count Gregorio Stenoff—a gentleman of noble pedigree it is true, but one of the most reckless dissipated rascals in Russia..." Follow the delicious but neglected Nadia as she works to wring every drop of pleasure out of life—despite an unhappy marriage. A classic title providing a peek into the secret sexual lives of another time and place. $5.95/267-1

THE STORY OF A VICTORIAN MAID   *Nigel McParr*

What were the Victorians really like? Chances are, no one believes they were as stuffy as their Queen, but who would have imagined such unbridled liberties! One maid is followed from exploit to smutty exploit! $5.95/241-8

CARRIE'S STORY   *Molly Weatherfield*

"I had been Jonathan's slave for about a year when he told me he wanted to sell me at an auction. I wasn't in any condition to respond when he told me this..." Desire and depravity run rampant in this story of uncompromising mastery and irrevocable submission. $5.95/228-0

CHARLY'S GAME   *Bren Flemming*

Charly's a no-nonsense private detective facing the fight of her life. A rich woman's gullible daughter has run off with one of the toughest leather dykes in town—and Charly's hired to lure the girl back. One by one, wise and wicked women ensnare one another in their lusty nets! $4.95/221-3

ANDREA AT THE CENTER   *J.P. Kansas*

Lithe and lovely young Andrea is, without warning, whisked away to a distant retreat. There she is introduced to the ways of the Center, and soon becomes quite friendly with its other inhabitants—all of whom are learning to abandon restraint in their pursuit of the deepest sexual satisfaction. $5.95/324-4

ASK ISADORA   *Isadora Alman*

An essential volume, collecting six years' worth of Isadora Alman's syndicated columns on sex and relationships. Alman's been called a "hip Dr. Ruth," and a "sexy Dear Abby," based upon the wit and pertinence of her advice. Today's world is more perplexing than ever—and Isadora Alman is just the expert to help untangle the most personal of knots. $4.95/61-0

THE SLAVES OF SHOANNA   *Mercedes Kelly*

Shoanna, the cruel and magnificent, takes four maidens under her wing—and teaches them the ins and outs of pleasure and discipline. Trained in every imaginable perversion, from simple fleshly joys to advanced techniques, these students go to the head of the class! $4.95/164-0

MASQUERADE BOOKS

A TITIAN BERESFORD READER

Beresford's fanciful settings and outrageous fetishism have established his reputation as modern erotica's most imaginative and spirited writer. Wild dominatrixes, perverse masochists, and mesmerizing detail are the hallmarks of the Beresford tale—and encountered here in abundance. The very best scenarios from all of Beresford's bestsellers. **$4.95/114-4**

CHINA BLUE

KUNG FU NUNS

"When I could stand the pleasure no longer, she lifted me out of the chair and sat me down on top of the table. She then lifted her skirt. The sight of her perfect legs clad in white stockings and a petite garter belt further mesmerized me. I lean particularly towards white garter belts." China Blue returns! **$4.95/3031-8**

HARRIET DAIMLER

DARLING • INNOCENCE

In *Darling*, a virgin is raped by a mugger. Driven by her urge for revenge, she searches New York in a furious sexual hunt that leads to rape and murder. In *Innocence*, a young invalid determines to experience sex through her voluptuous nurse. Two critically acclaimed novels in a special volume, available only from Masquerade! **$4.95/3047-4**

AKBAR DEL PIOMBO

SKIRTS

Randy Mr. Edward Champdick enters high society—and a whole lot more—in his quest for ultimate satisfaction. For it seems that once Mr. Champdick rises to the occasion, nothing can bring him down. Rampant ravishment follows this libertine wherever he goes! **$4.95/115-2**

DUKE COSIMO

A kinky romp played out against the boudoirs, bathrooms and ballrooms of the European nobility, who seem to do nothing all day except each other. The lifestyles of the rich and licentious are revealed in all their glory. Lust-styles of the rich and infamous! **$4.95/3052-0**

A CRUMBLING FAÇADE

The return of that incorrigible rogue, Henry Pike,who continues his pursuit of sex, fair or otherwise, in the most elegant homes of the most debauched aristocrats. No one can resist the irrepressible Pike! **$4.95/3043-1**

PAULA

"How bad do you want me?" she asked, her voice husky, breathy. I shrank back, for my desire for her was swelling to unspeakable proportions. "Turn around," she said, and I obeyed....This canny seductress tests the mettle of every man who comes under her spell—and every man does! **$4.95/3036-9**

ROBERT DESMOND

PROFESSIONAL CHARMER

A gigolo lives a parasitical life of luxury by providing his sexual services to the rich and bored. Traveling in the most exclusive circles, this gun-for-hire will gratify the lewdest and most vulgar sexual cravings! This dedicated pro leaves no one unsatisfied. **$4.95/3003-2**

THE SWEETEST FRUIT

Connie is determined to seduce and destroy Father Chadcroft. She corrupts the unsuspecting priest into forsaking all that he holds sacred, destroys his parish, and slyly manipulates him with her smoldering looks and hypnotic aura. The ultimate destructive seductress! **$4.95/95-5**

MASQUERADE BOOKS

MICHAEL DRAX

SILK AND STEEL

"He stood tall and strong in the shadows of her room... Akemi knew what he was there for. He let his robe fall to the floor. She could offer no resistance as the shadowy figure knelt before her, gazing down upon her. Why would she resist? This was what she wanted all along...." $4.95/3032-6

OBSESSIONS

Victoria is determined to become a model by sexually ensnaring the powerful people who control the fashion industry: Paige, who finds herself compelled to watch Victoria's conquests; and Pietro and Alex, who take turns and then join in for a sizzling threesome. $4.95/3012-1

LIZBETH DUSSEAU

TRINKETS

"Her bottom danced on the air, pert and fully round. It would take punishment well, he thought." A luscious woman submits to an artist's every whim—becoming the sexual trinket he had always desired. $5.95/246-9

THE APPLICANT

"Adventuresome young woman who enjoys being submissive sought by married couple in early forties. Expect no limits." Hilary answers an ad, hoping to find someone who can meet her needs. Beautiful Liza turns out to be a flawless mistress; with her husband Oliver, she trains Hilary to be submissive. $4.95/306-6

SPANISH HOLIDAY

She didn't know what to make of Sam Jacobs. He was undoubtedly the most remarkable man she'd ever met.... Lauren didn't mean to fall in love with the enigmatic Sam, but a once-in-a-lifetime European vacation gives her all the evidence she needs that this hot man might be the one for her.... A tale of romance and insatiable desires, this is one holiday that may never end! $4.95/185-3

CAROLINE'S CONTRACT

After a life of repression, Caroline goes out on a limb. On the advice of a friend, she meets with the alluring Max Burton—a man more than willing to indulge her fantasies of domination and discipline. Caroline soon learns to love his ministrations—and agrees to a very *special* arrangement.... $4.95/122-5

MEMBER OF THE CLUB

"I wondered what would excite me.... And deep down inside, I had the most submissive thoughts: I imagined myself ... under the grip of men I hardly knew. If there were a club to join, it could take my deepest dreams and make them real. My only question was how far I'd really go?" A woman finally goes all the way in a quest to satisfy her hungers, joining a club where *really* pays her dues—with any one of the many men who desire her! $4.95/3079-2

SARA H. FRENCH

MASTER OF TIMBERLAND

"Welcome to Timberland Resort," he began. "We are delighted that you have come to serve us. And...be assured that we will require service of you in the strictest sense. Our discipline is the most demanding in the world. You will be trained here by the best. And now your new Masters will make their choices." A tale of sexual slavery at the ultimate paradise resort. $5.95/327-9

RETURN TO TIMBERLAND

It's time for a trip back to Timberland, the world's most frenzied sexual resort! Prepare for a vacation filled with delicious decadence, as each and every visitor is serviced by unimaginably talented submissives. These nubile maidens are determined to make this the raunchiest camp-out ever! $5.95/257-4

MASQUERADE BOOKS

SARAH JACKSON

SANCTUARY

Tales from the Middle Ages. *Sanctuary* explores both the unspeakable debauchery of court life and the unimaginable privations of monastic solitude, leading the voracious and the virtuous on a collision course that brings history to throbbing life. $5.95/318-X

HELOISE

A panoply of sensual tales harkening back to the golden age of Victorian erotica. Desire is examined in all its intricacy, as fantasies are explored and urges explode. Innocence meets experience time and again. $4.95/3073-3

JOYCELYN JOYCE

PRIVATE LIVES

The illicit affairs and lecherous habits of the illustrious make for a sizzling tale of French erotic life. A wealthy widow has a craving for a young busboy; he's sleeping with a rich businessman's wife; her husband is minding his sex business elsewhere! $4.95/309-0

CANDY LIPS

The world of publishing serves as the backdrop for one woman's pursuit of sexual satisfaction. From a fiery femme fatale to a voracious Valentino, she takes her pleasure where she can find it. Luckily for her, it's most often found between the legs of the most licentious lovers! $4.95/182-9

KIM'S PASSION

The life of a beautiful English seductress. Kim leaves India for London, where she quickly takes upon herself the task of bedding every woman in sight! One by one, the lovely Kim's conquests accumulate, until she finds herself in the arms of gentry and commoners alike. $4.95/162-4

CAROUSEL

A young American woman leaves her husband when she discovers he is having an affair with their maid. She then becomes the sexual plaything of various Parisian voluptuaries. Wild sex, low morals, and ultimate decadence in the flamboyant years before the European collapse. $4.95/3051-2

SABINE

There is no one who can refuse her once she casts her spell; no lover can do anything less than give up his whole life for her. Great men and empires fall at her feet; but she is haughty, distracted, impervious. It is the eve of WW II, and Sabine must find a new lover equal to her talents. $4.95/3046-6

THE WILD HEART

A luxury hotel is the setting for this artful web of sex, desire, and love. A newlywed sees sex as a duty, while her hungry husband tries to awaken her to its tender joys. A Parisian entertains wealthy guests for the love of money. Each episode provides a new variation in this lusty Grand Hotel! $4.95/3007-5

JADE EAST

Laura, passive and passionate, follows her husband Emilio to Hong Kong. He gives her to Wu Li, a connoisseur of sexual perversions, who passes her on to Madeleine, a flamboyant lesbian. Madeleine's friends make Laura the centerpiece in Hong Kong's infamous underground orgies. Slowly, Laura descends into the depths of depravity. Steamy slaves—for sale! $4.95/60-2

RAWHIDE LUST

Diana Beaumont, the young wife of a U.S. Marshal, is kidnapped as an act of vengeance against her husband. Jack Beaumont sets out on a long journey to get his wife back, but finally catches up with her trail only to learn that she's been sold into white slavery in Mexico. $4.95/55-6

MASQUERADE BOOKS

THE JAZZ AGE

The time: the Roaring Twenties. A young attorney becomes suspicious of his mistress while his wife has an fling with a lesbian lover. *The Jazz Age* is a romp of erotic realism from the heyday of the speakeasy. $4.95/48-3

AMARANTHA KNIGHT

THE DARKER PASSIONS:
THE FALL OF THE HOUSE OF USHER

The Master and Mistress of the house of Usher indulge in every form of decadence, and are intent on initiating their guests into the many pleasures to be found in utter submission. But something is not quite right in the House of Usher, and the foundation of its dynasty begins to crack.... $5.95/313-9

THE DARKER PASSIONS: *FRANKENSTEIN*

What if you could create a living, breathing human? What shocking acts could it be taught to perform, to desire, to love? Find out what pleasures await those who play God.... $5.95/248-5

THE DARKER PASSIONS: *DR. JEKYLL AND MR. HYDE*

It is an old story, one of incredible, frightening transformations achieved through mysterious experiments. Now, Amarantha Knight explores the steamy possibilities of a tale where no one is quite who—or what—they seem. Victorian bedrooms explode with hidden demons. $4.95/227-2

THE DARKER PASSIONS: *DRACULA*

"Well-written and imaginative, Amarantha Knight gives fresh impetus to this myth, taking us through the sexual and sadistic scenes with details that keep us reading.... This author shows superb control. A classic in itself has been added to the shelves." —*Divinity* $5.95/326-0

ALIZARIN LAKE

THE EROTIC ADVENTURES OF HARRY TEMPLE

Harry Temple's memoirs chronicle his amorous adventures from his initiation at the hands of insatiable sirens, through his stay at a house of hot repute, to his encounters with a chastity-belted nympho—and many other exuberant and over-stimulated partners. $4.95/127-6

EROTOMANIA

The bible of female sexual perversion! It's all here, everything you ever wanted to know about kinky women past and present. From simple nymphomania to the most outrageous fetishism, all secrets are revealed in this look into the forbidden rooms of feminine desire. $4.95/128-4

AN ALIZARIN LAKE READER

A selection of wicked musings from the pen of Masquerade's perennially popular author. It's all here: *Business as Usual, The Erotic Adventures of Harry Temple, Festival of Venus,* the mysterious *Instruments of the Passion,* the devilish *Miss High Heels*—and more. $4.95/106-3

MISS HIGH HEELS

It was a delightful punishment few men dared to dream of. Who could have predicted how far it would go? Forced by his sisters to dress and behave like a proper lady, Dennis finds he enjoys life as Denise much more! Crossdressed fetishism run amuck! $4.95/3066-0

THE INSTRUMENTS OF THE PASSION

All that remains is the diary of a young initiate, detailing the twisted rituals of a mysterious cult institution known only as "Rossiter." Behind sinister walls, a beautiful young woman performs an unending drama of pain and humiliation. Will she ever have her fill of utter degradation? $4.95/3010-5

MASQUERADE BOOKS

FESTIVAL OF VENUS

Brigeen Mooney fled her home in the west of Ireland to avoid being forced into a nunnery. But the refuge she found in the city turned out to be dedicated to a very different religion. The women she met there belonged to the Old Religion, devoted to the ways of sex and sacrifices. $4.95/37-8

PAUL LITTLE

THE DISCIPLINE OF ODETTE

Odette's family was harsh, but not even public humiliation could keep her from Jacques. She was sure marriage would rescue her from her family's "corrections." To her horror, she discovers that Jacques, too, has been raised on discipline. A shocking erotic coupling! $5.95/334-1

THE PRISONER

Judge Black has built a secret room below a penitentiary, where he sentences the prisoners to hours of exhibition and torment while his friends watch. Judge Black's House of Corrections is equipped with one purpose in mind: to administer his own brand of rough justice! $5.95/330-9

TUTORED IN LUST

This tale of the initiation and instruction of a carnal college co-ed and her fellow students unlocks the sex secrets of the classroom. Books take a back seat to secret societies and their bizarre ceremonies in this story of students with an unquenchable thirst for knowledge! $4.95/78-5

DANGEROUS LESSONS

A compendium of corporeal punishment from the twisted mind of bestselling Paul Little. Incredibly arousing morsels abound: *Tears of the Inquisition, Lust of the Cossacks, Poor Darlings, Captive Maidens, Slave Island*, even the scandalous *The Metamorphosis of Lisette Joyaux*. $4.95/32-7

THE LUSTFUL TURK

The majestic ruler of Algiers and a modest English virgin face off—to their mutual delight. Emily Bartow is initially horrified by the unrelenting sexual tortures to be endured under the powerful Turk's hand. But soon she comes to crave her debasement—no matter what the cost! $4.95/163-2

TEARS OF THE INQUISITION

The incomparable Paul Little delivers a staggering account of pleasure and punishment. *"There was a tickling inside her as her nervous system reminded her she was ready for sex. But before her was...the Inquisitor!"* Unquestionable, one of Little's most torturous titles. $4.95/146-2

DOUBLE NOVEL

Two of Paul Little's bestselling novels in one spellbinding volume! *The Metamorphosis of Lisette Joyaux* tells the story of an innocent young woman initiated into a new world of lesbian lusts. *The Story of Monique* reveals the sexual rituals that beckon the ripe and willing Monique. $4.95/86-6

CHINESE JUSTICE AND OTHER STORIES

Chinese Justice is already a classic—the story of the excruciating pleasures and delicious punishments inflicted on foreigners under the tyrannical leaders of the Boxer Rebellion. One by one, each foreign woman is brought before the authorities and grilled. Scandalous tortures are inflicted upon the helpless females by their relentless, merciless captors. $4.95/153-5

SLAVES OF CAMEROON

This sordid tale is about the women who were used by German officers for salacious profit. These women were forced to become whores for the German army in this African colony. The most perverse forms of erotic gratification are depicted in this unsavory tale of women exploited in every way possible. One of Paul Little's most infamous titles. $4.95/3026-1

MASQUERADE BOOKS

ALL THE WAY

Two excruciating novels from Paul Little in one hot volume! *Going All the Way* features an unhappy man who tries to purge himself of the memory of his lover with a series of quirky and uninhibited women. *Pushover* tells the story of a serial spanker and his celebrated exploits in California. $4.95/3023-7

CAPTIVE MAIDENS

Three beautiful young women find themselves powerless against the wealthy, debauched landowners of 1824 England. They are banished to a sexual slave colony, and corrupted by every imaginable perversion. $4.95/3014-8

SLAVE ISLAND

A leisure cruise is waylaid, finding itself in the domain of Lord Henry Philbrock, a sadistic genius, who has built a hidden paradise where captive females are forced into slavery. The ship's passengers are kidnapped and spirited to his island prison, where the women are trained to accommodate the most bizarre sexual cravings of the rich, the famous, the pampered and the perverted. $4.95/3006-7

MARY LOVE

MASTERING MARY SUE

Mary Sue is a rich nymphomaniac whose husband is determined to pervert her, declare her mentally incompetent, and gain control of her fortune. He brings her to a castle where, to Mary Sue's delight, she is unleashed for a veritable sex-fest! $5.95/351-1

THE BEST OF MARY LOVE

Mary Love leaves no coupling untried and no extreme unexplored in these scandalous selections from *Mastering Mary Sue, Ecstasy on Fire, Vice Park Place, Wanda,* and *Naughtier at Night.* $4.95/3099-7

ECSTASY ON FIRE

The inexperienced young Steven is initiated into the intense, throbbing pleasures of manhood by the worldly Melissa Staunton, a well-qualified teacher of the sensual arts. Soon he's in a position—or two—to give lessons of his own! Innocence and experience in an erotic explosion! $4.95/3080-6

NAUGHTIER AT NIGHT

"He wanted to seize her. Her buttocks under the tight suede material were absolutely succulent—carved and molded. What on earth had he done to deserve a morsel of a girl like this?" $4.95/3030-X

RACHEL PEREZ

ODD WOMEN

These women are lots of things: sexy, smart, innocent, tough—some even say odd. But who cares, when their combined ass-ettes are so sweet! There's not a moral in sight as an assortment of Sapphic sirens proves once and for all that comely ladies come best in pairs. $4.95/123-3

AFFINITIES

"Kelsy had a liking for cool upper-class blondes, the long-legged girls from Lake Forest and Winnetka who came into the city to cruise the lesbian bars on Halsted, looking for breathless ecstasies...." A scorching tale of lesbian libidos unleashed, from an uncommonly vivid writer. $4.95/113-6

CHARLOTTE ROSE

A DANGEROUS DAY

A new volume from the best-selling author who brought you the sensational *Women at Work* and *The Doctor Is In.* And if you thought the high-powered entanglements of her previous books were risky, wait until Rose takes you on a journey through the thrills of one dangerous day! $5.95/293-0

MASQUERADE BOOKS

THE DOCTOR IS IN

"Finally, a book of erotic writing by a woman who isn't afraid to get down—and with deliciously lavish details that open out floodgates of lust and desire. Read it alone ... or with somebody you really like!"

—Candida Royalle

From the author of the acclaimed *Women at Work* comes a delectable trio of fantasies inspired by one of life's most intimate relationships. Charlotte Rose once again writes about women's forbidden desires, this time from the patient's point of view. $4.95/195-0

WOMEN AT WORK

Hot, uninhibited stories devoted to the working woman! From a lonesome cowgirl to a supercharged public relations exec, these women know how to let off steam after a tough day on the job. Includes "A Cowgirl's Passion," ranked #1 on Dr. Ruth's list of favorite erotic stories for women! $4.95/3088-1

SYDNEY ST. JAMES

RIVE GAUCHE

Decadence and debauchery among the doomed artists in the Latin Quarter, Paris circa 1920. Expatriate bohemians couple with abandon—before eventually abandoning their ambitions amidst the intoxicating temptations waiting to be indulged in every bedroom. $5.95/317-1

THE HIGHWAYWOMAN

A young filmmaker making a documentary about the life of the notorious English highwaywoman, Bess Ambrose, becomes obsessed with her mysterious subject. It seems that Bess touched more than hearts—and plundered the treasures of every man and maiden she met on the way. $4.95/174-8

GARDEN OF DELIGHT

A vivid account of sexual awakening that follows an innocent but insatiably curious young woman's journey from the furtive, forbidden joys of dormitory life to the unabashed carnality of the wild world. Pretty Pauline blossoms with each new experiment in the sensual sex. $4.95/3058-X

ALEXANDER TROCCHI

THONGS

"...In Spain, life is cheap, from that glittering tragedy in the bullring to the quick thrust of the stiletto in a narrow street in a Barcelona slum. No, this death would not have called for further comment had it not been for one striking fact. The naked woman had met her end in a way he had never seen before—a way that had enormous sexual significance. My God, she had been..." Trocchi's masterpiece—unexpurgated! $4.95/217-5

HELEN AND DESIRE

Helen Seferis' flight from the oppressive village of her birth became a sexual tour of a harsh world. From brothels in Sydney to harems in Algiers, Helen chronicles her adventures fully in her diary. Each encounter is examined in the scorching and uncensored diary of the sensual Helen! $4.95/3093-8

THE CARNAL DAYS OF HELEN SEFERIS

Private Investigator Anthony Harvest is assigned to save Helen Seferis, a beautiful Australian who has been abducted. Following clues in Helen's explicit diary of adventures, he Helen, the ultimate sexual prize. $4.95/3086-5

WHITE THIGHS

A fantasy of obsession from a modern erotic master. This is the story of Saul and his sexual fixation on the beautiful, tormented Anna. Their scorching passion leads to murder and madness every time they submit to their lusty needs. Saul must possess Anna again and again. $4.95/3009-1

MASQUERADE BOOKS

SCHOOL FOR SIN

When Peggy leaves her country home behind for the bright lights of Dublin, her sensuous nature leads to her seduction by a stranger. He recruits her into a training school where no one knows what awaits them at graduation, but each student is sure to be well schooled in sex! $4.95/ **89-0**

MY LIFE AND LOVES (THE 'LOST' VOLUME)

What happens when you try to fake a sequel to the most scandalous autobiography of the 20th century? If the "forgers" are two of the most important figures in modern erotica, you get a masterpiece, and THIS IS IT! One of the most thrilling forgeries in literature. $4.95/**52-1**

MARCUS VAN HELLER

TERROR

Another shocking exploration of lust by the author of the ever-popular *Adam & Eve*. Set in Paris during the Algerian War, *Terror* explores the place of sexual passion in a world drunk on violence. $5.95/**247-7**

KIDNAP

Private Investigator Harding is called in to investigate a mysterious kidnapping case involving the rich and powerful. Along the way he has the pleasure of "interrogating" an exotic dancer named Jeanne and a beautiful English reporter, as he finds himself enmeshed in the crime underworld. $4.95/**90-4**

LUSCIDIA WALLACE

KATY'S AWAKENING

Katy thinks she's been rescued after a terrible car wreck. Little does she suspect that she's been ensnared by a ring of swingers whose tastes run to domination and unimaginably depraved sex parties. With no means of escape, Katy becomes the newest initiate into this sick private club—much to her pleasure! $4.95/**308-2**

FOR SALE BY OWNER

Susie was overwhelmed by the lavishness of the yacht, the glamour of the guests. But she didn't know the plans they had for her. Sexual torture, training and sale into slavery! $4.95/**3064-4**

THE ICE MAIDEN

Edward Canton has ruthlessly seized everything he wants in life, with one exception: Rebecca Esterbrook. Frustrated by his inability to seduce her with money, he kidnaps her and whisks her away to his remote island compound, where she emerges as a writhing, red-hot love slave! $4.95/**3001-6**

DON WINSLOW

THE MANY PLEASURES OF IRONWOOD

Seven lovely young women are employed by The Ironwood Sportsmen's club for the entertainment of gentlemen. A small and exclusive club with seven carefully selected sexual connoisseurs, Ironwood is dedicated to the relentless pursuit of sensual pleasure. $5.95/**310-4**

CLAIRE'S GIRLS

You knew when she walked by that she was something special. She was one of Claire's girls, a woman carefully dressed and groomed to fill a role, to capture a look, to fit an image crafted by the sophisticated proprietress of an exclusive escort agency. High-class whores blow the roof off! $4.95/**108-X**

GLORIA'S INDISCRETION

"He looked up at her. Gloria stood passively, her hands loosely at her sides, her eyes still closed, a dreamy expression on her face ... She sensed his hungry eyes on her, could almost feel his burning gaze on her body...." $4.95/**3094-6**

ORDERING IS EASY!

MC/VISA orders can be placed by calling our toll-free number

PHONE 800-375-2356 / FAX 212 986-7355

or mail this coupon to:

MASQUERADE BOOKS
DEPT. Y74A, 801 2ND AVE., NY, NY 10017

BUY ANY FOUR BOOKS AND CHOOSE ONE ADDITIONAL BOOK, OF EQUAL OR LESSER VALUE, AS YOUR FREE GIFT.

QTY.	TITLE	NO.	PRICE
			FREE
			FREE

Y74A

SUBTOTAL	
POSTAGE and HANDLING	
TOTAL	

We Never Sell, Give or Trade Any Customer's Name.

In the U.S., please add $1.50 for the first book and 75¢ for each additional book; in Canada, add $2.00 for the first book and $1.25 for each additional book. Foreign countries: add $4.00 for the first book and $2.00 for each additional book. No C.O.D. orders. Please make all checks payable to Masquerade Books. Payable in U.S. currency only. New York state residents add 8¹/⁴% sales tax. Please allow 4-6 weeks delivery.

NAME_____

ADDRESS_____

CITY_____ STATE _____ ZIP_____

TEL( )_____

PAYMENT: ☐ CHECK ☐ MONEY ORDER ☐ VISA ☐ MC

CARD NO. _____ EXP. DATE _____